# SONG OF THE FIANNA

## WARRIORS OF THE FIANNA
## BOOK ONE

BY
SOPHIA NYE

## ARE YOU SIGNED UP FOR DRAGONBLADE'S BLOG?

You'll get the latest news and information on exclusive giveaways, exclusive excerpts, coming releases, sales, free books, cover reveals and more.

Check out our complete list of authors, too!

No spam, no junk. That's a promise!

### Sign Up Here

www.dragonbladepublishing.com

*Dearest Reader;*

*Thank you for your support of a small press. At Dragonblade Publishing, we strive to bring you the highest quality Historical Romance from some of the best authors in the business. Without your support, there is no 'us', so we sincerely hope you adore these stories and find some new favorite authors along the way.*

*Happy Reading!*

*CEO, Dragonblade Publishing*

# Additional Dragonblade Books by Author Sophia Nye

**Warriors of the Fianna Series**
Song of the Fianna (Book 1)
Prince of Fire (Book 2)

# THE WARRIORS OF THE FIANNA

Deep in the heart of the Kingdom of Munster, the legendary King Brian Boru has brought an ancient brotherhood back to life: The Fianna. Now entering his senescence, King Brian has all but achieved his dream of becoming High King of Éire, uniting the nine kingdoms to defend Éire's emerald shores from *Fin Gall* raiders. He will need the aid of the kingdom's best warriors to complete his vision and claim the seat of the High King.

But it is no simple task to become a warrior of the Fianna. Seven trials, the same seven used by the ancient Fianna, test the mettle of all who would claim such an honor.

*Intelligence:* Memorize the twelve books of poetry, that you may be knowledgeable on the history, genealogy, and legends of your people.

*Defense:* With naught but staff and shield, defend yourself from nine men's spears while standing deep in a hole.

*Speed:* Outrun pursuers through a forest, without being injured. But take care! Not a branch may be broken to prove your skill.

*Movement:* Leap over a tree with a height to match your own, then crawl beneath a branch lower than your knee.

*Recovery:* Run through the forest with all speed until you step upon a thorn. Remove it, but don't slow down!

*Bravery:* Fight outnumbered without faltering.

*Chivalry:* Marry for love.

*Truth in our hearts,*
*Strength in our arms,*
*Honesty in our speech.*

# PROLOGUE

*Monastery at Cill Dara, Éire, AD 999*

IT HAD BEEN, thus far, the worst year of her entire life. Eva sighed deeply, setting down her white feather quill on the ink-stained table and placing her hands on her throbbing temples.

What little remained of the pale sunlight struggled to reach her workspace. The copying building, hardly larger than her own quarters had been back home, held all the materials necessary for the sisters of St. Brigit to transcribe important documents. Eva's eyes pained her from straining so long in the failing light.

First her betrothed had died. The *first* of her betrotheds died, she corrected herself, sending a silent prayer heavenward for their souls. They'd both gone, one after the other. Duncan had died fighting a war that need never have begun—a war he only joined because of her. Her second betrothed's death was no accident of battle. Nay, her devil of a cousin had done the deed himself, a murderer and traitor if ever there was one. If that were all, then that would be something. But, alas, it only worsened from there. And it was all her fault.

Abbess Miriam appeared before Eva could wander down the darker turns of her mind, looking none too pleased.

"What's the trouble?" Eva stood to greet the woman with a respectful bow.

Abbess Miriam rolled her lips inward, as though keeping in the words might render them untrue. "You have—*guests*."

Eva's heart beat faster than a bodhrán, hammering like wood

against hide.

Abbess Miriam was a well-bred woman from a respected family. There was only one reason she'd refer so ungraciously to Eva's visitors.

They must be from her aunt's side of the family.

Picking up her woolen habit, Eva made haste out of the cramped building. It took her eyes a moment to adjust after walking out of the dark cave of a room in which she'd spent the afternoon. When she started toward the hall, where guests were received, the abbess halted her.

"They're in the infirmary."

Eva felt the color drain from her face. The battle. She'd known it was coming, she'd feared it for so long. Tensions, stoked, no doubt, by her wretched cousin Baeth, had steadily risen over the past months. It seemed they'd finally bubbled over like an untended pot.

"Sitric?" Eva guessed, changing direction and hurrying toward the infirmary.

"And his men. They're making the others uncomfortable."

Of course, they were. No one trusted the Ostmen, foreigners from the far north who had been raiding the shores of Éire for generations. They'd managed to carve out settlements along the coast, though the natives of Éire had fought mightily against such a travesty. Her cousin, Sitric, was king of one such settlement— Dyflin. "How badly is he wounded?"

"He'll live," Abbess Miriam grumbled, "but I don't want them staying past the morn."

Before Eva could reply, they'd reached the infirmary's double doors. It wasn't a large building, enough for five cots and a small hearth, the sisters of Cill Dara had learned long ago that hauling an injured man inside was a far easier task with wider doors.

The acrid smell of blood and sweat had Eva covering her nose the moment she entered. Six giant Ostmen sat piled up inside the small stone building.

"Cousin!" Sitric stood, covered in blood, and embraced her.

Eva pulled back to examine him, unable to believe that he could move given the amount of blood he must have lost.

"'Tis not mine," he assured her. "Mostly."

"He's only suffered a nasty gash on his leg," Abbess Miriam explained, her arms crossed tightly. She perched in the doorway, glaring at Sitric.

"What's happened? Did Brian come for Dyflin?"

Sitric nodded, looking down at his booted feet. Silent.

"Sitric," Eva begged, "what aren't you telling me?"

"There's no easy way to say this," he mumbled, "so I'll just out with it. It wasn't only Brian. He came with allies, a force far greater than just his own men. Your father…" His voice trailed off tellingly.

Eva steeled herself. She could see precisely where this was headed. To the bitter end she'd expected all along. "What of my father?"

"I'm so sorry, Eva." His voice was soft, his Ostman accent giving an endearing lilt to his words of comfort. "He tried to divide their army, but instead was swallowed by it. I couldn't get to him."

"Conn mac Murrough was a good man," Abbess Miriam declared from the doorway. "I shall go and pray for his soul." With a sad smile for Eva, the abbess departed toward the chapel.

"Eva." Sitric's gentle tone only unsettled her more.

"My brother," she stammered, managing to piece together the words amidst her shock. "What of Dallan?"

"Your brother lives," Sitric assured her. He spoke in the Ostman language, something they'd done often as children when she stayed in their home. That he did it now meant he spoke of important matters, which he didn't want overheard. "I'm afraid the bad news doesn't end with your father's death. You'd best fetch us some dinner and ale. We've a long night ahead of us."


By the time the last streaks of orange had disappeared below the horizon, Eva found herself sitting beneath the great oak tree next to Sitric, sharing a meal of smoked salmon and leeks. A chill breeze captured the last of the bronze leaves overhead, their rhythmic rattling sending a feeling of foreboding through Eva. Sitric's men supped inside the infirmary, tending the last of their flesh wounds and licking their even more wounded pride.

It didn't take a fool to guess that Sitric had lost Dyflin. He'd yet to tell her the extent of it, but Eva knew enough to know the situation was dire.

"I need your help," he said, handing her a choice bite of salmon. "You are one of the few I trust."

When he didn't elaborate, Eva decided to get to the heart of it. "What of Astrid? And your mother?" Sitric's younger sister Astrid, Eva's dearest friend and cousin, had not been married off yet. Which meant that both she and her mother had likely been in Dyflin when it was attacked.

"Brian has them," Sitric admitted quietly. "He and Malachy took the city. I was too wounded, had lost too many of my men. Your father was gone. I couldn't find Uncle Morda or Baeth. I fled, knowing I could help them more if I lived than if I died."

Eva took a moment to process it all.

Brian Boru had been trying for years to claim the title of High King of all Éire. Her cousin Sitric and her Uncle Morda were two of the kings who hadn't accepted him as their overlord. With them as allies, he had only to defeat the current High King, Malachy. Now they had little choice, it would seem.

One part of his tale surprised Eva, however. "Malachy fought with him? I thought they were at war?"

Sitric grinned at that, rather unexpectedly. "I angered them when I raided north along the coast," he boasted. "So much so that enemies became allies."

Of course, her cousin would be proud of such a feat.

"I told you not to do that," Eva chided.

Sitric shrugged. "I had my reasons."

"And now they have Astrid."

That sobered him. "Aye," he answered. "And we must get

her back."

"We?"

"Though I despise him, my mother assures me that Brian is an honorable man, if annoying. I have come to ask you to play the part of the hostage in our negotiation."

"Why me?" Eva asked in shock. "I'm hardly a valuable hostage. And isn't it typical to send a man, not a woman?"

Sitric grinned at her wickedly. "It is indeed."

Understanding dawned, followed quickly by indignation. "You wish to use me to insult the man?"

"Precisely."

"And *precisely* how is insulting the man holding your kingdom, your sister, and your mother captive going to improve the situation?"

Sitric ran a hand along his blonde braids. The *Fin Gall*, the fair foreigners. That was what the natives of Éire called the invaders from the north. In Eva's estimation, it was an apt descriptor. The *Fin Gall* tended to have fair or red hair with pale blue eyes—a stark contrast to the dark hair and green eyes so typical of those born on the island. Though there was variation, she herself one such example, Eva found it held some truth.

"You're the niece of one king, cousin of another, and daughter of a prince. All of whom fought in the battle for Dyflin. And, most importantly, you're dear to me. Brian knows this. He knows how close our kin are. He'll be insulted that I offer a woman, aye, but he'll see the reason behind it also."

Eva breathed deeply of the night air surrounding them. First her mother, now her father. Both men she'd been meant to marry had died as well. Everyone dear to her found an early grave, it would seem. The least she could do was keep Astrid and her aunt alive for now.

"I'll do it. For Astrid. And Aunt Gormla."

Sitric chuckled. "For Astrid, anyway," he agreed. "Brian wouldn't dare cross my mother. I think he's terrified of her."

"What, that she'll marry him again?" Eva tried to joke on the matter but found her mind wandering toward her impending captivity.

"Precisely," he added merrily. "The very threat of it would keep him at bay." Then his mirth faded and he took her hands in his own. "It won't be forever, Eva. Just until I have enough men to fight back."

"It could be ten years, Sitric," Eva reminded him, thinking of other noble hostages she'd heard of in tales.

"Which is why it must be you. Astrid and your brother will want families and children, and they'll be busy with that soon I imagine. You want neither."

"And if he kills me?"

A dark cloud descended over her cousin's fair features. "Then I kill him, king or not."

# CHAPTER ONE

*Cenn Cora Fortress, Éire, AD 1000*

FINN HAD THE distinct sensation that he was being taken advantage of by his new companion. Dallan had shown up at a curiously opportune moment, insisting he needed Finn's help, and proceeded to convince Finn to follow him to King Brian's fortress at Cenn Cora.

Obviously, Finn wouldn't have been foolish enough to follow a complete stranger to almost-certain death under normal circumstances. But after watching his future turn to ash before his very eyes, Finn was willing to take a few chances. Besides, he could hold his own in a fight if it came to it.

"How'd it go?" Finn asked as Dallan returned to their campsite in the woods just outside Cenn Cora.

Dallan grinned broadly, the happiest Finn had seen him since they met two days ago. "Better than expected. It's a good thing you're here, though. He wants me to speak with her only tomorrow morn and under guard, so we can't plot anything insidious. Honestly, I don't know whether I ought to be flattered or insulted."

Finn lifted his pack onto his shoulders. "Flattered. Definitely," he offered. "He sees you as a genuine threat."

"And as a man who would break a peace treaty, steal a hostage, and endanger my cousins."

"Fair enough," Finn replied evenly. "Let's not do any of that, then, eh?"

Dallan only shrugged before leading them back the way he'd come, toward the great hall at Cenn Cora.

Once again, Finn's good sense twinged in warning at Dallan's noncommittal response. The man plotted more than he let on, but what, precisely, Finn couldn't guess.

Finn knew Dallan's young sister was being held hostage by the King Brian of Mumhain, and that Dallan had every intention of seeing her freed. His plan, as far as Finn could gather, was to participate in a series of trials and become one of Brian's most trusted warriors, one of the Fianna, in order to barter for the girl's freedom.

"You still haven't told me how it is you think I can help," Finn reminded him as they walked.

The fortress stood on a tall hill, gilded in emerald trees and overgrown brush. The sun settled into the horizon behind it, golden rays swirling with darkening shadow as they picked their way through the dense forest.

Dallan was quiet a bit too long but sounded sincere when he finally answered. "I need you to be me," he explained, his voice tinged with sadness. "Eva is delicate. She's young. She's still grieving the loss of our parents, and no doubt worried over her future. But I'm not to speak with her, check up on her to see to her happiness. Let her know she'll be going home soon. I need you to do that for me. I'll send her messages through you, and you can bring hers to me."

It sounded far too simple. "And explain to me again why it is you needed me, and only me, for this position as your messenger?"

Dallan stopped walking to look Finn dead in the eyes. "I know it seems unlikely, but I spoke with about a hundred people over the past weeks since I learned of Brian's Fianna trials. You're the only one who can do everything I need."

Finn sighed and kept walking. That was about as much of an answer as he'd ever gotten from Dallan. He liked the man, truly, but he didn't know a damned thing about him.

He'd gathered that Dallan must be wealthy, from an important noble family if his sister was deemed an acceptable hostage for the king of such a prominent kingdom. Likely he wasn't on good terms with the king either, given the circumstances. Beyond that, Finn knew precious little about the man who had seemingly taken over his life.

"Alright," Dallan announced, as they neared the edge of the forest, the sound of merriment spilling out from the hilltop before them, "I'll go first. You follow along in an hour or so. If Brian knows you came with me, he won't let you near Eva either."

Finn nodded, entirely uncertain about the whole affair. He didn't have a lot of options, however, now that he'd failed his family. He couldn't face them after what happened, not before he'd found something good to tell them along with the bad. Dallan had convinced him to undergo the trials alongside him. Who knew? Maybe in seven months' time Finn could go home and tell his parents he was a member of the King Brian's most elite warrior band, performing tasks for the most powerful man in the nine kingdoms. Or he'd be dead after failing said trials. Either was preferable to nothing at all.

The hour felt as long as ten. Finn listened to the revelry in the hall, ignoring the grumbling of his own stomach. He was going to have words with Dallan if he missed dinner entirely, though it wouldn't be the first time he'd gone hungry.

Finally, he climbed the last half-mile of hillside and threw open the doors of the hall. He instantly regretted being the one to arrive second.

Everyone, all hundred or more of them, stopped to look at the latecomer. Finn felt a flush of embarrassment color his cheeks, but gave them a look that dared any to question him. It was all a bluff, of course. A quick scan of the room told him he was likely poorer than even the serving wenches. Flashes of gold, silver, and jewels caught his eyes from every table.

He took in the room as he searched for Dallan. It was a massive round hall, the sort he'd expect of a man of Brian Boru's position. Layers of beams and rafters held candle-filled chandeliers and overcrowded trestle tables. The entire room smelled of roasted boar, sweat, and smoke. The jaunty music of a skillfully played whistle floated above the murmur of conversation, but Finn couldn't find the bard playing it. A dancing fire filled a pit in the center of the building. The king and queen sat atop a dais directly opposite the fire from Finn.

And at their feet beneath the dais sat the saddest, most beautiful woman he'd ever seen.

Finn's breath caught as he watched her, unable to tear his gaze away yet knowing he ought to do just that. She was an Ostwoman, wearing a red and blue apron dress with golden brooches. Everything she wore paled in comparison to her, however.

Her long-braided hair couldn't quite decide its color, shifting from brown to gold in the flickering firelight. Pouty pink lips reminded him of a flower in snow, accentuated by her cream complexion. He couldn't tell the color of her eyes, but he was shocked by how much he wanted to discover it.

Though he was taken aback by her obvious beauty, what struck Finn most about her was her absent stare, as though she looked at the room before her yet saw none of it. He couldn't help but wonder what might have happened to leave her so distant from those around her. In his experience, being an Ostman was enough to condemn one to a life as an outsider. Perhaps, like him, she felt such a sting from her heritage.

As he stood staring, contemplating approaching her to learn more, her gaze finally wandered to him. At first, she retained that absent, distant look. Finn smiled at her, hoping he might raise her spirits.

He knew the moment she saw him—really *saw* him. Her eyes filled with a clear warning—a warning to keep away.

They were a deep shade of green.

Normally, her response would only have pushed Finn closer to her out of sheer curiosity. What was going through her mind?

But this eve he must instead find Dallan, for he knew his companion needed him. With great reluctance, he tore himself from her fierce challenge, finally spotting Dallan several tables away.

"Is there room for another?" he asked, sliding onto the bench next to Dallan, pretending he didn't know him at all.

"Aye," Dallan answered, along with a few of the other men, "have a seat."

"I'm afraid you've missed the feast," said a man seated opposite him. The fellow had deep golden hair streaked with pale brown, much darker than Finn's, that reached his shoulders. He was a beast of a man with an air of command about him, the sort Finn would expect to find at the trials for the Fianna. "I'm Illadan," he offered, extending his hand in greeting.

"Finn." He took it, trying to place the name. His vast knowledge of the noble families of Mumhain, learned for his poet training, failed him momentarily, though Illadan's name struck familiar.

Dallan slid him a platter of roasted boar, carrots, and leeks with a few slices of bread, casting him a sideways grin. "I couldn't quite finish mine. You're welcome to what's left."

Finn might not trust Dallan, but he had never been more grateful for a platter of food. He thanked Dallan and dove straight into his dinner.

"Illadan here is Brian's nephew," Dallan explained as Finn ate.

Finn paused, finally remembering where he'd heard Illadan's name. "You're Mahon's son," he thought aloud. "I've sung songs of your victory near Dyflin."

Illadan smiled wryly, looking at Dallan as he spoke. "I assure you, the songs were more pleasant than the experience."

"Well fought, either way," Finn declared, ignoring the odd looks between his two companions. Though he wasn't well-versed in the politics of nobles, even Finn realized that King Brian had ordered Illadan to sit with Dallan to keep an eye on him. In fact, he'd wager Illadan would be around them quite a lot in the following months.

Illadan nodded at the small lap-sized harp tied to Finn's pack. "Have you trained with the masters?"

Finn chewed the bite of boar he'd just taken slowly, buying himself a few moments to collect his thoughts. He knew folk would be asking since, according to the legends, poetry and music were among the trials of the Fianna. He just hadn't decided how to answer yet. His heart still felt raw over the rejection he'd received not a fortnight earlier.

"Not formally." It was as good as he could do for now.

"Spoken like a man with talent he won't admit," Illadan replied with amusement. "I look forward to hearing you play."

They exchanged similar pleasantries until Finn's plate lay empty and men started to trickle out of the hall. Illadan had proven a formidable dinner companion, asking interesting questions and giving vague answers of his own. When their table was nearly empty save for Finn, Dallan, and Illadan, the king's nephew leaned forward. "Are you *Fin Gall?*" he whispered to Finn.

Finn's pulse quickened, his mouth drying up like a stream during a drought. He was forevermore fighting his heritage. "My father," he mumbled. He'd hoped it wouldn't matter again, but clearly he'd been wrong.

Illadan nodded, crossing his arms pensively. "I'd not mention that to Brian," he replied. "If you prove yourself, he won't care. But in the meantime, I'd keep that private."

"And if he observes as keenly as you?" Finn countered. He could hardly hide his resemblance to his father, who looked painfully foreign.

"Lie," Illadan advised without hesitation. "As a poet, you well know his entire family was killed by the foreigners. I doubt he'll ever forget it. Now," he said louder, "if you'll excuse me, I believe I shall retire for the evening. It's been a pleasure."

"That went well, I thought," Dallan muttered under his breath.

Finn began to voice his agreement when movement near the dais caught his attention. The Ostwoman walked purposefully out a side door, looking stricken as ever. Finn couldn't name the source of his concern for her, but he felt deeply that she needed help. Beside him, Dallan tensed.

"Go after her," he whispered.

Finn turned to look at his companion. "The Ostwoman?"

Dallan's lips flattened, his jaw tightening noticeably. "She's no Ostwoman," he growled. "She's my sister."

# CHAPTER TWO

Eva hurried out the door—away from Brian, away from humiliation. As a hostage, Eva Nic Murrough, Princess of Laigin no longer existed, replaced instead by a nameless Ostman noble, the embodiment of King Sitric's submission to the king. This was doubly ridiculous and humiliating, as she looked nothing like her Ostmen cousins and didn't have a drop of foreign blood to her. Aye, her hair was a touch lighter than most natives of Éire, but nothing like the bright red and gold locks of her Ostmen relatives. Her cousin Astrid's hair looked ready to catch fire at any moment.

Yet at every feast, at every public event, at every visit of every noble since she became Brian's hostage, Eva was made to look like she'd been born offshore. So everyone could see that Sitric Silkbeard, an Ostman, had submitted to Brian Boru.

Her cousin, Astrid, had embroidered the hem of the deep blue apron dress with intricate knotwork, a blend of their two heritages. Her Aunt Gormla had sewn the red tunic, worn beneath the apron, specially for Eva for her visits to Dyflin. On her fifteenth birthday, nearly ten years ago now, Sitric had presented her with golden brooches, to wear with beads across her chest. Until her time as a hostage, it had been one of her favorite dresses, a symbol of love from those dearest to her.

Now, it pained her to wear it.

Though she'd only been at Cenn Cora for a sennight, Eva's feet knew well the path down to Loch Derg. Branches and worn stones sent gentle pressure into the soles of her lightly slippered feet.

Eva wanted to be strong for her family, for her beloved cousins, for her brother. But with each passing day she felt her strength waning. It became harder and harder to look toward her future, if indeed she even had one. Eva's spirits drifted steadily downward. Of late, the only way she could keep herself afloat was to stand at the water's edge, watching the waves lap the stone-filled sand. She let her thoughts wander like the currents at her feet.

Emptiness consumed her. She stood on the lakeshore, a river of tears flowing into the vast expanse of water before her. Broken and alone, she poured her heartache into each wrenching breath she took.

She missed each one so terribly. The names and faces of those she'd loved and lost haunted her every waking moment.

*Duncan.* Her first betrothed. Five years past.

*Oran.* Her second betrothed. Three years past.

*Sheeva.* Her mother. Six months past.

*Conn.* Her father. Four months past.

There were those, too, who hadn't left this world behind but were still lost all the same. She knew, deep in her weary bones, she *knew* she'd never see them again.

*Gormla.* Her aunt.

*Sitric.* Her cousin.

*Astrid.* Her cousin. Her dearest friend and confidante.

Every day she wandered alone to the shore to grieve. And every day she herself died a little more.

An owl hooted across the water. A second answered from just overhead. At least not everyone was alone.

Her heart faltered at that thought. She wasn't exactly alone anymore, but she wasn't certain her brother endangering his life on her behalf counted as any sort of victory. Brian had summoned her just before the feast to tell her all about her foolish brother's bid for her freedom, at the cost of his own. She would do whatever was necessary to talk sense into him.

Yet there existed a small, selfish part of her that hoped he might have seen her leave and follow her down to the water. She hadn't spoken with Dallan since their mother had died six months ago. It would raise her spirits immeasurably to spend time with him again.

The sound of footfalls on the path behind her brought a hitch to her breath. Had he come after all?

She turned, watching the path that emptied from the forest to the lakeshore, hardly able to breathe as she awaited her unexpected visitor.

Her short-lived hopes came crashing down when a stranger emerged.

It wasn't Dallan.

It was the man who'd been staring at her shamelessly almost as soon as he'd entered the feasting hall. She'd scowled at him then, attempting to deter any forward ideas he might have, but even that hadn't worked straightaway. Nevertheless, she scowled at him again as he approached, not trying in the least to hide her disappointment at his appearance.

He paused, regarding her as she glared at him menacingly, but only for a moment. Then he kept walking toward her across the shadowed clearing.

Eva was trapped. Whatever this man wanted, he'd surely get it for she had no way to defend herself. He was the largest man she'd ever seen. Even if she called for help, she wasn't certain she'd be heard so far from the hall. At least not in time to be saved.

She backed toward the lake, prepared to throw herself in if, at any point, that would be to her advantage. Though, admittedly, she'd prefer not to since she couldn't swim.

He did stop then, several paces from her. "I'm not here to harm you," he assured her softly. "I need to speak with you."

Eva didn't trust him. "What could you possibly need to say to me? I don't even know you."

The man bit his bottom lip, as though considering his options. He looked around them, back to the path and along the shore. Then he whispered. "Your brother sent me."

It took Eva several hesitant breaths before she realized that he'd spoken in *Norrøna*, the language of the Ostmen. The language of her cousins. Only her parents and Dallan knew she spoke it, having learned it while she fostered in Dyflin.

If Dallan had sent someone instead of following her himself, he must be in more danger than she'd realized.

"Why did he send *you*?" she answered in the same tongue, still wary of the complete stranger she now found herself trapped with alone.

The man moved slowly, taking one step at a time until he stood two arm-lengths from her at the edge of the water. In the light of the waxing moon, she saw him clearly enough. He sat down, removing his bag and his sword, then laid on his back with his hands behind his head, facing the night sky.

Showing her he was no threat. And that he wasn't leaving any time soon.

Eva followed his lead, sitting down and pulling her knees toward her chest, wrapping her arms about them protectively. She thought he'd forgotten her pointed question entirely until his deep, rich voice uttered a gentle answer.

"He is worried about you," he told her, still speaking *Norrøna*. "The king won't let him see you for fear of treachery. I am to take word from you to him, act as messenger. When we speak of your brother, we should use the foreign tongue."

"Don't you think that would be equally suspicious?" she countered skeptically. None of this sounded like a good idea.

He shrugged. "Better than they know for certain what we say. From what your brother has told me, the king isn't overly fond of him."

"Better he not defy the king at all," Eva retorted. "Did my brother send a message? Or are you here for no reason other than introducing yourself? Which, I might point out, you've yet to do."

"Your tongue is nearly as sharp as my sister's," he chuckled, turning his head to look at her. "I am Finn."

"Son of?"

"Ulf."

She heard the hesitation in his response, his voice barely audible over the lapping waves. "You're an Ostman?"

"Half of one, aye."

Eva's curiosity was piqued, for outside her relatives in Dyflin, she'd not met any other Ostmen. She'd certainly never met any who weren't of noble lineage. It explained how he knew their language.

Finn didn't give her a chance to ask anything further. "Dallan wanted me to tell you that he plans to free you, and you shouldn't worry over him."

"I don't want him to," she hissed. "I'll not have him trade his life for my own. I chose this so that he wouldn't have to."

He sat up, his arms supporting his giant frame as he leaned back in the damp sand. "You chose to be a hostage?"

"Someone had to do it," Eva explained. "Sitric came to me for help, and I knew it would be better for me to go with Brian than my cousin or my brother."

"Your brother seems to disagree."

Sensing this may be her only chance to stop Dallan's nonsense before it went too far, Eva moved closer to Finn, pleading with her eyes as she spoke. "You *must* make him leave. If he becomes a hostage, he may never be king. I won't have him give up his future for me."

Finn stilled at her words. "King?" His voice was low, dangerous. "King of *what*?"

"He didn't tell you who he was?" Eva had trouble believing that. She loved her brother dearly, but he erred on the side of boastful to be sure. "How did he convince you to help him then?"

Finn ran a hand over his face, worrying his bottom lip again.

Eva had been too distracted by his massive size and intentions earlier to notice that he was also incredibly handsome. But now that she sat beside him, somewhat placated, she could clearly see his chiseled jaw that looked as though a master stonemason had carved it. His blue eyes reminded her of the waters of the lake beside them, myriad shades that were smooth on the surface, but held untold depth beneath. The tan on his skin spoke of time spent outdoors. His hair was the color of sand, a pale, mottled gold.

"He told me his sister had been taken hostage and he had a plan to free her but needed help to see it through. Obviously, as we traveled, he told me more of you and a bit of his plan. But not once did he mention his parentage, nor did I ask. I assumed he was some lesser noble's son. Not a king's."

Eva smiled sadly. "He's a king's nephew and a king's grandson," she told him, taking pity. "Our father was never a king."

"Will you tell me which kingdom, lady?"

"Laigin."

Finn swore under his breath.

In his shoes she'd likely have done the same. Until the battle in Dyflin, Laigin had been one of the kingdoms still fighting against Brian's reign as high king.

Though King Morda of Laigin and King Sitric of Dyflin had taken nominal oaths of allegiance and offered Eva as a hostage, few, including Brian himself, believed the conflict concluded. Her kin were stubborn folk, with no desire for an over-king. Particularly Sitric.

"I suppose I ought to be grateful he had me enter separately. Else we'd both have been run through if it went poorly."

Her chest tightened on his behalf. How like her brother to keep something so important from the very man helping him. Dallan could be so obtuse. Eva reached out to him, placing her hand over his on the cold sand. "If it helps, he probably thought that the less you knew, the safer you'd be."

His eyes wandered to her hand, his fingers flexing under her touch. "Or he thought I would abandon him should I learn the truth of what dangers lie ahead."

"My brother can be foolhardy," Eva admitted, holding his gaze, "but he doesn't trust easily. If he believed you the sort to run at the first sign of trouble, he wouldn't have brought you at all."

He stood, pulling his hand free and offering it to help her up. "Let me walk you back to the keep."

"I'll be fine on my own, thank you." She didn't want to risk being seen coming back from the lake alone with a man, particularly one so handsome as Finn. Though it wasn't so frowned upon to have trysts before marrying as it was in other parts of the world, Eva had no interest in raising gossip. She had had enough embarrassment to last a lifetime already.

"I'm sure you'd be safe, my lady," he replied. "But it seems to me you lack for company."

It was a presumptuous thing to say, even if it were true. A fluttering in her belly, nerves most likely, made Eva agree anyway. "Only to the forest's edge," she muttered, leading the way back up the hillside quietly plotting how she might end her brother's ridiculous ploy.

No matter how despondent she grew in her solitude, Eva chose this life so that others need not. She wasn't about to stand by and watch while anyone—foolhardy brothers included—suffered on her account. But how could she keep her brother from seeing his plan through?

# CHAPTER THREE

FINN WATCHED EVA make her way across the hilltop and into the row of lodgings near the keep, wondering what he'd just gotten himself into. When Dallan had talked of his sister, Finn got the distinct impression that she was still a child of fostering age, younger than fifteen summers to be sure.

He had not expected a woman full-grown. And certainly not a woman so beautiful and captivating as Eva. Something about her plucked at his heart like a harp string and, though he was none too pleased with Dallan at the moment, Finn found himself grateful that he might be able to help Eva shed whatever sadness had overcome her.

Over fifty warriors had come to participate in Brian's trials. Though Cenn Cora boasted a spacious keep and numerous outbuildings, the king couldn't possibly fit so many men in its walls. In the valley at the base of the hill, a makeshift village of tents had been set up to accommodate the warriors.

When Finn returned to his tent, he found Dallan waiting for him. And he found his own patience running low.

"So when did you plan to tell me you were the nephew of Brian's sworn enemy?" he asked darkly.

"I see you had a nice chat with my sister." Dallan stood, crossing his arms and pacing. "I didn't want to risk your safety any more than necessary."

"Do you think me a coward?" Finn couldn't hide his frustration. "Or simply that I cannot be trusted?"

"If I thought either of those things, you wouldn't be here," he shot back. "The less you know, the better. Though, I admit, that was rather a large omission."

"Is there anything else I ought to know?" Finn replied, sitting heavily on his cot. "Are you married to a princess? Is your cousin the pope?"

"My cousin is the King of Dyflin. Sitric."

Finn looked askance at him. "The Ostman who raided Cenn Lis?"

"Yes, well," Dallan looked uncomfortable for the first time since they'd met. "Eva and I both told him it was a terrible idea."

Finn wasn't quite sure what to say to that, finding himself caught somewhere between shock, horror, and curiosity. What must Dallan's life have been like before now? He could hardly imagine.

Dallan walked over and sat beside him. "What did Eva say?" he asked, his voice filled with concern. "Is she alright? She looked so miserable at dinner."

"I think she's lonely," Finn explained. He knew well how it felt to belong somewhere, yet not be wanted all the same. You could be surrounded by folk, yet still feel more alone than if you were the only person there. In the deep sadness in her eyes, the way she didn't speak to a soul, rushing off after dinner to stare pensively into the water—in all of it Finn saw a mirror of his own bleak thoughts.

Dallan rubbed his chin, considering Finn's statement. "I'm sure they're ignoring her mostly. And she's probably still upset over father's death."

Dallan had never mentioned that. "I'm so sorry," Finn told him.

"Four months ago," he offered. "At the battle."

"The one Sitric lost, forcing him to give Eva as a hostage."

Dallan's jaw clenched. "The very same."

"She doesn't want you to save her, Dallan." Finn knew it had to be said. He remembered the desperate look in her eyes when she'd told him as much.

"Of course, she doesn't. But it's my responsibility to see to her safety, now that our father's gone. Letting her spend the best years of her life rotting in Brian's keep as a trophy is not part of my plan."

"She said you'd be giving up the kingship," Finn added. He felt compelled to do justice to her argument, since Eva couldn't be here to deliver it herself. "And that she chose to be here."

Dallan shrugged. "Hostages aren't kept forever," he replied. "There's a good chance I'll be freed before my uncle dies. And, if not, I'd rather have my sister live her life than be king for a month. You and I both know 'tis rare to enjoy so long a kingship as Brian."

"You see her in the morning?" Finn asked.

"Aye. But then not again."

"If I were you, I'd sort this out with her then," Finn advised. "I don't think I'll be able to resolve it by going between the two of you."

Dallan nodded reluctantly, rising to take his leave. "I believe you might be right, my friend. Thank you for your help tonight. We'll speak on it more tomorrow."

He left without another word, leaving Finn wondering what else they could possibly discuss. It seemed like a matter between Dallan and Eva, and Finn had no interest whatsoever in getting tied up in family squabbles. Particularly in so powerful a family.

EARLY THE FOLLOWING morn, Eva was summoned to the great hall. She found King Brian and Dallan clearly in the midst of a contest to see who could look more furiously at the other.

Illadan, King Brian's dashing nephew, reclined at a table near the smoldering fire in the center of the hall.

"I'll take my leave," the king told Dallan. "Don't be late." He brushed past Eva on his way out the door, gracing her with a greeting so brief she wondered if he'd even spoken.

Eva rushed to her brother, wrapping him in the tightest hug she could manage, given that her arms couldn't possibly reach around him. Tears fell against her best efforts, forcing her to sniffle and wipe her eyes.

"Eva." Dallan sounded so worried she could hardly bear it. He wiped her cheek tenderly. "Everything will be fine," he assured her. "I'm here to take care of you."

"It's so good to see you." Her voice was the thinnest whisper, fragile even to her ears. "But you must leave. I'm just fine, and I won't have you risking your life to be the hero I don't need."

He chuckled. "Such a warm greeting," he teased. "And I'm not going anywhere. We're family. And you don't have to do this alone."

"Something tells me that even if you stay, I will still be alone," Eva replied softly. He wouldn't have sent Finn otherwise. As refreshing as it had been to have a meaningful conversation with someone other than the owls near the lake, Eva wasn't about to put her brother at risk over a few lonely tears. "You don't need to *buy* friends for me," she hissed, quiet enough that she doubted Illadan could hear.

Dallan hugged her tighter so that he could whisper in her ear. "I'm not paying him. And you do need a friend. If I could visit with you, you know I would."

Eva pulled away. "I have ladies' maids," she told him.

"That's not the same, and you know it."

She did know it. But she wasn't about to admit it. She needed to convince him that she was fine or else he'd never give up his attempted rescue. "I'm managing Cenn Cora in Queen Dunla's absence," she told Dallan. "I'll be plenty busy making sure fifty-two men have meals each day and a healer when they inevitably need one."

"Fifty-three," Dallan corrected her.

Eva put her hands on her hips, summoning all her strength to push past the ache in her chest at the thought of being alone again. "Fifty-two. You'll be leaving."

His eyes, filled with determination, locked with hers. "Not for a long time."

Illadan rose from his seat near the fire. "I wish I could give you both longer," he said, walking over to join them, "but the king's party needs to leave soon. We must be there for his speech."

Eva frowned pointedly at her brother as they accompanied Illadan out to the courtyard. She wasn't about to give in so easily. Everyone who grew close to her ended up dead, and Eva would throw herself into the lake before she let anything happen to Dallan.

# CHAPTER FOUR

FINN STOOD AMONG the crowd of men gathered in the grass-covered courtyard, listening as King Brian explained what was expected of them.

"I am old," he began. "And my kingdom is growing beyond my reach. If we are to keep this land safe, we must stand united against further invasion. I have spent my life working toward such an end, but there are those who yet resist my bid for peace."

At this, the king looked pointedly toward Dallan and Eva, who stood near the front of the crowd. Finn felt his chest contract in sympathy. He'd not want to be singled out by Brian, particularly for dissent.

"In order to see my vision of a united Éire realized, I am reinstating the ancient order of the Fianna. It will be as it was in the legends of old, from the trials for entry to the tasks I give the honorable few who survive. You will undergo the Seven Trials of the Fianna. Any who succeed at all seven will swear an oath of fealty to me and join my Fianna, to carry out quests across Éire and help to unite the nine kingdoms."

A roar of applause followed this statement. Finn gave a half-hearted cheer as he looked at the men around him. How many would still live in seven months' time? Were all these men here because they believed so deeply in Brian's cause that they were willing to give their lives for it? Or were some, like Finn, here because they had no better options in life?

As the cheering continued, the king, queen, and their retinue climbed into carriages, carts, and wagons to make their journey back to Caiseal, the ancestral seat of the kings of Munster. When he was gone from sight, Illadan addressed the crowd, flanked by two similarly burly men who looked of an age with him. Finn didn't recognize either of them, though he had no doubt he'd know them well by the time the trials concluded.

"Training will begin immediately," Illadan announced, calling the masses to attention once more. "We will spend a fortnight training and a fortnight of trials on each of the seven tasks. Any trials that take less than a fortnight to judge will give you more time to train for the next one."

"In seven months, we will have our Fianna to present to the king. I am Illadan, son of Mahon mac Kennedy and nephew of Brian Boru. This is Cormac, son of Cahill mac Conor mac Teague and Prince of Connachta. And this is Broccan, leader of the army of Brian Boru, soon-to-be High King of Éire. We will act as judges during the trials which will put to test your Intelligence, Defense, Speed, Movement, Recovery, Bravery, and Chivalry.

"You have a fortnight, beginning this day, to memorize and learn to perform the twelve books of poetry. Any who have had bardic or poetic training please come forward and speak with us. Good luck."

Finn couldn't stop himself from smiling. He'd had the twelve books memorized by the time he turned nine and had been performing them ever since. Though that hadn't been enough for the masters, he knew it would serve him well in his first task.

Perhaps eighteen years of training hadn't been wasted after all.

Feeling confident about his first trial, Finn made his way to Illadan, pushing past the other warriors as politely as he could. Five more men appeared beside him, some looking more comfortable than others. Glancing around, Finn noticed that Eva had disappeared at some point toward the end of the speeches. He wasn't sure why, but it disappointed him that she'd gone. Dallan, too, had wandered into the crowd behind him.

Illadan smiled warmly at him. "Finn! I was hoping you'd come up. Tell me truly, no plays at modesty. How are you with the twelve poems?"

Finn sighed. He wasn't particularly fond of drawing attention to himself, but he wasn't about to let Illadan down.

"I've been reciting them for sixteen years."

"Why are you not training with the masters?" Cormac, whom Illadan had introduced as a prince of Connachta, stepped forward to join the discussion.

"It's a long story," Finn replied, "and one I'm not as eager to tell." It was a horrendous understatement. He'd rather die in battle than discuss it with his own family, let alone two princes.

Illadan eyed him suspiciously but kept his own counsel.

"Come perform for us, and then you will help train the rest of the men."

"With respect," Finn added, "I doubt anyone could master the twelve poems in a fortnight."

"That's why it's a test of intelligence," Illadan answered evenly. "But we aren't looking to turn them into bardic masters in a fortnight. If they can memorize and recite the poems by then, it will prove the strength of their intellect. And if you can have them trained, it will prove the strength of yours."

"Every member of the Fianna must eventually master the bardic art, as is befitting so legendary a warrior," Cormac added. "But we recognize that true mastery will be achieved over time. We'd just like to see a good start for now."

Finn nodded. "I'll go fetch my harp."

"We'll be in the hall waiting," Illadan informed him, turning to address the other five men who'd approached as Finn took his leave.

Trying not to panic over finding a way to train fifty men in a fortnight, Finn returned to his tent.

Only to find Dallan waiting for him yet again.

"If you're courting me, you're doing a piss poor job of it," Finn remarked as he picked up his harp.

Dallan laughed, his eyes crinkling at Finn's jest. "You'd be so lucky," he retorted. "Anyway, I was thinking—"

"That's *never* good," Finn interrupted. "And I need to get to the hall."

Dallan waved away his concern with his hand. "I'll be quick. You should teach Eva to play."

That stopped Finn in his tracks. "Absolutely not." He couldn't discern why it seemed like such a bad idea, but he felt deep in his belly that he should avoid it.

"Think about it," Dallan pleaded. "It will give her something to distract her from her melancholy, and it will give her an opportunity to speak to someone often. She used to love learning the harp. I would do it myself if Brian allowed it."

"I will bring her your messages, and you hers," Finn argued, "but I think it would seem odd if I went out of my way to spend quality time with a hostage. And I imagine Illadan might be sour that I'm tutoring a captive princess instead of the men who have a trial in a fortnight."

Dallan grinned at that, approval written on his face. "He put you in charge of training them?" he asked. "Well done, my friend."

Finn sighed. "He *will* put me in charge of training them. *If* I meet him in the hall. Immediately."

"Fine," Dallan relented. "Take my sister a message after dinner, then."

"And what shall I tell her?"

"Ask her if she wants you to teach her to play the harp."

"You're an arse, you know that?"

"I'm also your best friend," Dallan countered.

Finn glared at him, but he couldn't deny the truth of Dallan's claim. He'd had precious few friends to begin with, and at this point Dallan knew him as well as any of them. He turned to head to the great hall, but not so fast that he missed Dallan's final words.

"Thank you, *best friend!*" he shouted, emphasizing the last bit.

As though guilt would work on Finn.

Finn swallowed hard, unable to lay aside the gnawing in his gut at leaving his friend to worry and Eva to misery. It would seem, for now, that guilt would indeed work.

# CHAPTER FIVE

FOLLOWING BRIAN'S SPEECH, Eva's morning had transformed into a frenzy of activity. Cenn Cora was a sizeable keep, requiring her near-constant attention. Grateful for the distraction, Eva threw herself into her work.

"Milady." The cook, this time.

Eva struggled to recall the name she'd heard during the whirlwind tour Queen Dunla had given her the day prior.

"Yes?" Lord, what was the woman's name?

"We're out of boar," she informed Eva hastily, as though it was the most embarrassing thing that could happen. "What shall I feed them?"

"Moira!" Eva exclaimed, pleased that she'd finally remembered the cook's name. "We have fifty-odd warriors camped outside. A hunt should be no trouble. I shall speak with Illadan and see it organized."

Moira nodded but continued to wring her hands in worry. "And for tonight?"

"Make a stew with whatever is left. If they go one night without meat it won't kill them. Make extra bread and pies for dessert."

Moira curtsied, taking her leave toward the steaming kitchens.

"And Moira?" Eva called, forcing the woman to turn back around.

"Aye, milady?"

"Next time tell me *before* we run out of stock."

"Of course, milady."

Eva turned away this time and couldn't keep from wondering if the servants were conspiring to set her up for failure. Surely, they too, didn't despise her on account of her family?

She strode across the courtyard, mainly grass with wagon ruts dug in, doing her best not to wrench an ankle on the uneven terrain. She wasn't certain where to find Illadan. He had as much, or more, to do than Eva, and could be needed just about anywhere.

She first poked her head into the keep proper, where the royal family resided, but found no sign of him. She continued down the row of buildings, coming next to the tower from which men kept watch for invaders. Still no sign of Illadan, but the guards thought he might be in the hall.

Eva reached the great hall, placing her hand on the door and nearly pushing it open. She stilled when she heard the sounds within, not daring to intrude yet unable to leave.

Someone was playing the harp. Nay, she corrected herself, the most talented bard she'd ever heard was coaxing a heavenly melody from the harp. It sounded effortless, and yet she'd never heard such a complex pairing of chords.

Taking two steps to the side, Eva leaned against the stone wall, letting the music carry her away. She was not prepared at all for the song that started up as an accompaniment, the first of the twelve poems. The words she'd heard a hundred times. Her parents and relatives had hosted master bards and poets at every feast they held. Yet not one of them had sounded so compelling.

The singer's deep, rich voice reminded her of the taste of honey in summer, coating her empty world in sweet warmth. He poured such emotion into his voice and his playing that Eva wondered if he had anything left after he finished a performance. It sounded as if his very spirit came to life in the music.

Realizing she'd lingered too long, Eva lifted herself off the wall, deciding she'd return when Illadan wasn't busy listening to the most amazing performance she'd yet witnessed.

As she hurried away from the hall, she heard the door open behind her. Unable to contain her curiosity, she turned to see none other than Finn heading back down the hill with a small harp.

For the first time in months, Eva smiled.

ALL THROUGH DINNER, Eva watched Dallan and Finn with feigned disinterest. Her heart ached every time Dallan laughed, which was often in the company of his new friend. He had the same smile as their father. Even his laugh held echoes of the man who'd been lost to them not so very long ago.

How could she convince him to leave? The last thing she wanted was one more person dying on her account. Yet it seemed so many were determined to do just that. Two engagements and one fallen father later, here she sat, making the best of a bad situation. At least as a hostage, she had thought, no one else would be in danger. Indeed, she might even be sparing someone else the trouble. She lifted a spoonful of thick stew partway to her mouth, deciding in the end she wasn't all that hungry. Mayhap if she died of starvation her brother would finally give up this foolish quest of his.

After most had finished their meals and the servants cleared the tables, Illadan stood, silencing the room with his raised hand. "Finn," he called, "sing us the tale of the seven trials."

Finn moved toward the dais, sparing a quick smile for Eva as he took the bard's seat near Illadan. Why it made her stomach flutter, she couldn't say.

She also couldn't say why, after having met him already, she suddenly noticed how well-muscled his arms were, especially for someone who had clearly spent more time playing the harp than fighting. She'd have to ask him about that the next time Dallan sent a message. Not his muscles, she reminded herself, just his training.

When he opened his mouth, pure magic followed. If she

hadn't known any better, she'd have said his father was one of the Fair Folk from the Otherworld, not from across the sea, so enchanting was his voice. Looking over the faces before her, Eva saw that she wasn't the only one enraptured by his performance.

He told the tale of the seven trials that Finn mac Cumhail put his Fianna through to test their abilities, the same trials the men gathered would soon endure themselves. She wondered if Finn had been named for the hero of old. If so, his parents must have a touch of the sight, she mused. When it ended, Eva felt as though she'd lost something she couldn't quite name, a feeling of completeness that had slipped away before she knew it was there.

First Illadan, followed abruptly by everyone else in the room, stood and applauded, shouting and whistling and begging for another tale. Eva couldn't fault them; she could listen to him sing the entire night.

Two songs later, Illadan finally allowed Finn a reprieve, dismissing the men to rest before their training resumed the following morn.

Eva's heart sank deeper in her chest as his final song drew to a close. She nodded to her brother, disappearing from the hall with haste to take up her post looking out over the moonlit lake.

Secretly hoping that for the second night in a row, she'd not be alone.

# CHAPTER SIX

S HE WASN'T EATING. Finn had kept track of every bite she took during the course of dinner. Not because he felt the need to intrude upon her privacy, but because the night prior he realized everyone else had finished eating and she'd not touched her food. Not even one bite taken from her bread.

Tonight, she'd done better than nothing, he supposed, but he wasn't satisfied with the paltry attempt she'd made. Three bites. That was all she'd taken of her dinner. Unless she was eating biscuits by the fistful in the morning, Finn didn't know how she'd survive to the end of the week on so little nourishment. Nor, indeed, how she'd survived for so long already.

Which is why, halfway through the meal, he began carefully setting aside the most portable parts of his own dinner, wrapping them in the cloth meant for wiping one's hands.

When he reached the lakeshore that Eva seemed to love so much, she spun to face him. If he didn't know any better, he'd say she even looked happy to see him.

"What's that?" she asked warily, eyeing the parcel of food he held.

He frowned at her. "The dinner you didn't eat." He sat beside her near the water, laying out the meal on top of the cloth.

Eva didn't move. "And how would you know how much I did or didn't eat?"

"I watched you," he replied, not bothering to explain any further.

"I don't need a nursemaid," she grumbled, sitting down on the other side of the cloth.

"But you do need food." He handed her a slice of bread. "And I'm not leaving until you've eaten all of this." She may not need a nursemaid, but she clearly needed company.

Her face softened as she took the bread from him. Pulling a miniscule piece from it, she popped it into her mouth. "You don't need to worry over me," she whispered when she'd finished chewing. "I'm fine."

"Well, that's a relief," Finn replied teasingly.

They sat together in silence as she ate slower than Finn had thought humanly possible. But he didn't have anywhere to be, other than resting, and she clearly *wasn't* fine. When she ate the last bite of cheese, he handed her the waterskin he carried on his belt.

She took it gratefully, drinking long and deep before handing it back. "Thank you," she muttered, as though embarrassed by the entire situation. "You didn't have to do that."

"I did," Finn argued. "And I will do the same as often as necessary."

"What message did my brother have for me?" she asked.

Finn had been so concerned over her eating that he'd forgotten he told her he'd be meeting with her only to relay messages. He cleared his throat, reluctant to do as Dallan had asked that morn.

"Is it so terrible?" she pressed when he said nothing.

"Dallan wishes me to teach you to play the harp."

He turned to look at her, catching the glimmer that came to her eyes at his suggestion. The hint of a smile played at the corners of her mouth.

"Really?" she asked breathlessly. Then, apparently having second thoughts, she cleared her throat. "I mean, I wouldn't want you to do it out of pity. I've had quite enough of that."

Finn watched her face fall as she spoke, wrenching his heart out of place. "It's not pity," he argued. "I want to do it." And he meant it. Aye, when Dallan suggested it, Finn hadn't cared for the idea. He couldn't put a name to his reasoning, but something about spending so much time with Eva put him on edge. But he quickly tossed aside his nameless worries when he realized how happy it would make Eva.

Her arms crossed her chest defiantly. "Is it not? Would you want to do it if my brother hadn't put you up to it?"

He considered her carefully before answering. He knew what he said mattered a great deal to her. "Your brother may have suggested it," he began, "but I would like to do anything that will bring a smile to your face. And that was as close as I've come so far."

She did smile then, her lips transforming into a full, taut bow. "That's not true, actually."

"No?"

A flush of pink invaded her creamy cheeks, reminding him once again of flowers blooming in snow. "Your music made me smile."

His chest swelled at her admission. "Then you shall hear it as often as you'd like." He'd had folk complimenting his talents since he was a child. Yet for some reason, knowing that he could raise her spirits and coax a smile from her troubled countenance felt like the highest praise he'd received.

"You play so well," she began, "yet you're here to fight. How can you have trained adequately for both?"

Finn grinned at her. "Worried I'll be speared to death, and you'll lose your music tutor?" he teased.

"The latter more than the former, for certain," she replied in kind. "But really, how can you have trained to play so perfectly and also learned to fight well enough for the trials?"

"'Tis true I studied music and poetry for most of my life," he admitted, "but my father and uncle are as fierce as any warriors you'll meet. They trained me well enough."

"May I ask a personal question?" she ventured.

"More personal than how I trained as a warrior?" He tried to sound as though it didn't matter, when in truth he avoided all discussion of his family. Which, based on her previous question, is where he wagered this was headed.

She nodded. "Your father and your uncle. What brought them here?"

Finn felt himself tense at the question. "Are you asking if my family plundered the island before settling?" He couldn't keep the edge from his voice.

Eva didn't back down, though he was clearly uncomfortable with the conversation. "My cousin has, so far, plundered no fewer than three monasteries and two towns," she reminded him gently. "And that's to say nothing of my extended family and their allies. Suffice it to say, I understand why Brian is cross with Sitric, though I love my cousin no less for it."

He hadn't considered that she herself had ties to the Ostmen who'd invaded Éire. He'd entirely overlooked that she was here because of those relatives. Of the many folk who'd asked him about his Ostman heritage, she was the only one who had no reason to hold it against him.

"My uncle came to Éire in his nineteenth summer on a *viking*," Finn told her. "He never returned. Two summers later my father, his older brother, came looking for him."

"Was he alright?" Eva scooted toward him on the sandy shore, concern written across her delicate features. "Did he find him?"

"Aye," Finn answered, growing more comfortable as his tale went on. "My father found my uncle all right. He had decided he'd rather be a tradesman than a *viking*, and started a shipping business in Luimneach. He'd not yet been able to send word home."

"And your father stayed as well? In Luimneach?"

Finn shook his head. "My father has always been a farmer, from his birth to the present. He loves working the land, living in villages where everyone knows each other's business," he said with a laugh. "And in one such town just south of Luimneach, called Ath Dara, he found my mother. They've been there since."

Eva smiled at him, filling him with warmth. "You've naught to be ashamed of, Finn," she assured him. "It sounds like a fine family you have, no matter whence they came."

"I'll try to remember that," he replied, surprised to find he meant it.

As he packed up the cloth and helped Eva to her feet, one thought played in Finn's mind over and over: he'd told the truth earlier.

He would do anything to see that smile.

# CHAPTER SEVEN

THE FOLLOWING MORN Eva woke with the sun. She was ashamed to admit that most days she lay in bed far longer than she ought, and with no good reason to do so. But not today.

Her first harp lesson with Finn was after dinner tonight, and it was all she could do to make it through the day in all her excitement. Though he'd made a good argument about not doing it out of pity, Eva still wasn't convinced that he'd have agreed had her brother not intervened. She reminded herself of this as often as possible to ensure she kept a level head throughout her day. She had a keep to run, after all. She could hardly afford to daydream about music.

"My lord!" she called, finally catching the evasive prince on his way across the courtyard. "Do you have a moment?"

Illadan strode toward her with a grin. Though he was quite tall, she thought Finn was taller still. "What do you need, my lady?"

"We need boars," she replied. "Moira informed me yesterday we'd run out, and I thought you might have men to spare for a hunt."

She stifled a giggle at the look of concern on his face. So much worry over a simple dish.

"We shall go today. Thank you for your assistance."

"'Tis my pleasure, my lord."

Though the day had begun well enough, by dinner Eva felt battered. A devastating fire in the kitchens left them functioning below what was needed to feed all the men. Eva had to make arrangements for a temporary kitchen to be set up, consisting mainly of a large fire pit in a vented tent and a massive table. Luckily, even if they were short a kitchen, the keep at Cenn Cora was anything but short-handed. Illadan sent five men to do the physical labor required, in addition to however many he had spared for the hunt.

Eva oversaw the project, somewhat disappointed when Finn was not among the men Illadan sent. She didn't know why she should be upset by it, particularly since she'd be seeing him in a few hours' time.

Finally, after what had become quite a trying day, the hour arrived for dinner. After the initial feast, she was no longer required to wear her apron dress, for which she was immensely grateful. Instead, she'd chosen a plain cream gown, well-fitted but understated. The last thing she wanted was to have men approaching her.

Even if she had any interest whatsoever in marriage, which she didn't, she doubted Brian would consent to her marrying as a hostage. She didn't dare to imagine Dallan's outrage if he discovered a man desired his little sister. Not that she foresaw that being a problem any time soon.

Eva took her spot at the foot of the dais, watching as the men arrived in the hall. A flutter like the susurrus of butterfly wings erupted deep in her belly when Finn entered. She smiled when he looked at her from across the room, for a moment forgetting everyone else entirely. Forgetting that her father had died, that she was a hostage. Forgetting, even, that she was alone.

The flutter turned into a gentle tug when he smiled back at her, a single dimple appearing on his cheek.

"You're happy tonight."

Eva reluctantly looked away from Finn, finding Illadan passing by on his way up the dais.

"I'm pleased we have roast boar again," she lied. She could hardly tell him what had actually brought a smile to her face.

"The men will perform better for it."

"I'm certain they will," he agreed. "Enjoy your dinner, my lady."

When servants set platters upon the tables, a general murmur of approval drifted through the room. It would seem one day without meat had been one day too many, Eva thought with amusement. She decided not to tell them yet that she wasn't going to serve it at all during Advent.

Eva tried to figure out what Dallan and Finn said to one another in conversation. As a hostage, she sat entirely alone and it provided at least mild entertainment. Halfway into the meal, Dallan started laughing infectiously, turning her thoughts once more to her father. What she wouldn't give for him to be here to see Dallan laughing, to share another meal with him herself.

In the midst of her mind's dark wanderings, Finn's deep blue eyes captured hers. It took her a moment to realize that he was frowning at her with abject disapproval.

She shrugged her shoulders and tilted her head, attempting to illustrate her utter loss as to why he should be cross with her.

His gaze darkened further. Without breaking eye contact, he roughly tore a sizeable chunk of bread from his trencher, waved it at her, and ate it.

She burst into laughter, unable to help herself. He looked like he wanted to murder her over a loaf of bread. And he looked none too pleased that she found his reminder amusing.

Now Dallan was looking at her as well, though he seemed to think she'd finally gone mad. She watched him nudge Finn, who shrugged and gave a short reply, before giving her yet another meaningful glare.

Deciding he'd more than earned it, she made a show of taking an obscenely large bite of her own bread. And determined that perhaps he had a point. Had it really been so long since she'd eaten a proper dinner? She didn't remember bread tasting so delectable before. Crusty and salty on the outside, warm and sweet on the inside. Much like her older brother, she thought wryly. She'd have to save that barb for their next meeting.

The thought led directly to one which was far more serious. As much as Eva wanted to verbally spar with her brother like they had as children, she wanted him safe even more. And she still hadn't found a way to convince him to leave.

The meal was followed with a performance by one of the other bards, a lean warrior with dark, wild curls. He played beautifully, but Eva doubted anyone could play like Finn. It wasn't a fair comparison.

And she couldn't be happier about getting lessons from him, though she'd never admit it to Dallan. The last thing he needed was to see the bottomless depths of her desperation.

The very moment it was seemly, Eva made her way down to Loch Derg. Unable to sit, she paced before the water's frothy edge. The full moon cast the water in a sheen of silver, like a blade melted in the hottest forge. Across the lake, the owl began its nightly conversation with her companion overhead.

"Do you ever swim?"

Eva turned, her breath catching as she watched Finn walk over to her in the quicksilver moonlight, his harp strung over his shoulder. He certainly was handsome. She laughed, partly to distract him from her momentary lapse of thought at his appearance and partly at his ridiculous question. "I can't swim."

His glare returned, his eyes like storm clouds rolling across blue skies. "Let me get this straight." He released each word with great effort, working his jaw while he spoke. "You come alone. At night. To the lake. And *you can't swim?*"

Eva did her best not to laugh, rolling her lips together. "It's not as though I'm going to simply tumble into the water," she said, attempting to pacify him. "I assure you, I'm perfectly safe."

"Your brother should have taught you," he growled.

Deep in her core, it felt as though someone had plucked a bow, or perhaps pulled it tight. Either way, it was unsettling. "Swimming is for men to learn and women to watch." She repeated the phrase her brother had told her every time she'd asked to learn.

Finn was even less amused, if that were possible. He ran a hand through his golden hair, heaving a put-upon sigh.

"What?" she asked, feigning ignorance of his discomfort.

"Just how many men have you watched swimming?"

"Why Finn Ulfsson," she teased, walking in front of him with a sidelong glance, "if I didn't know any better, I'd say you were jealous."

He scoffed. "I'm not, I assure you. I'm merely concerned that you're learning improper form by watching fools paddle about." He grabbed her arm as she passed him, gently but firmly. "Promise me you won't come down here without me."

"Finn," she began, but he shook his head.

"Promise," he demanded.

"Fine," she agreed, trying not to think about how much she liked the feel of his grip on her arm.

"Good. Now then, let's play the harp, shall we?"

# CHAPTER EIGHT

FINN HADN'T THE faintest idea how he was going to get through this lesson, let alone all the other ones she'd be expecting. When he first walked onto the shore, breaking out from under the canopy of trees, she'd looked painfully beautiful, pacing the shore alone in the moonlight. The dress she wore hugged all her curves—the ones he wasn't supposed to notice on Dallan's little sister. And, best of all, she'd smiled when she saw him.

Then, of course, she had to go and admit that she was far more foolish than he'd thought possible. How could she come here alone, to a *lake*, and not know how to swim? How did she not see the danger in it?

He'd stopped himself from falling down a hole, imagining how many trips she'd made here already, how many chances she'd already had to drown. Gods, he was grateful he'd asked. At least now he could ensure her safety.

He sat in the usual spot, where he'd laid the cloth of food for her the night before and pulled his harp into his lap.

She did the same, folding her legs beneath her and sitting so close he could feel her there without looking. "Can I touch it?" she asked, reaching for his lap.

For a singular moment, Finn forgot she spoke of his harp. He cleared his throat, nodding, but unable to answer. He was only here to teach her to play, to keep her company in Dallan's stead, he reminded himself sternly. And he'd only be doing so during the trials. If he failed a trial, he'd be gone or dead. And if, by some miracle, he and Dallan survived to the end, Eva would be sent home. Their time together would be but brief, and he couldn't spoil it by wreaking havoc on both their hearts.

She ran her fingers over the instrument reverently, caressing first the body carved of elm and willow, then the brass strings strung tightly between. "It's beautiful," she breathed. "Where did you get it?"

"My parents." She was coming too close to something he had no desire to speak of, even with Eva.

Something in his answer made her look up at him, away from the harp. "It makes you sad."

It wasn't a question.

"They spent too much on something I didn't need with money they didn't have." With money they ought to have used on something far more important.

Eva leaned closer to him, her eyes the color of sun-drenched fields in summer and filled with as much warmth. "I have heard masters from every one of the nine kingdoms, the best bards according to all who hear them. Not a one of them could sing or play as you do. You have a gift, and your parents were right to give you a harp to match it."

Finn's eyes stung at her sincerity. She had no idea how nearly she'd come to bringing up the most painful part of it all. *A harp fit for a master bard*, they'd said when they gave it to him. Master bard, indeed.

"I'm going to teach you to play correctly," he told her, desperate to change the subject. "When you pick up a harp, the instinct is to pull the string like an arrow and release it, like this." He showed her, plucking a single string.

She nodded. "'Tis how I play it. Is that wrong?"

"Was a master teaching you?" he asked, unable to hide his frustration.

When she nodded, a surge of anger gripped his stomach. "He taught you wrong."

"Why wouldn't a master know how to play it correctly?"

"Oh," Finn growled, unable to hide his disgust, "he knew how to play correctly. He just didn't teach *you* to play correctly."

Eva shook her head, confusion writ on her face. "But why would he do such a thing?"

"Because you're a woman."

"That's ridiculous," she objected, still shaking her head. "Master Kerrill wouldn't do that."

"He would," Finn argued, "and he did. Most masters don't believe women capable of learning to play the harp with proper technique. It's nonsense, to be sure, but 'tis what they say."

He watched determination take over Eva. She readjusted her position, sitting straighter and giving Finn a look so smoldering he had to turn away before his mind strayed too far. "Show me."

"The proper way is not to pluck them, but to tap them. It makes a richer, fuller sound with better range. Like this." He hit a string with one of his nails, almost flicking it but with more control. "To string multiple notes together without losing them in each other, you use your other hand to stop the string from vibrating."

"May I try?"

He handed her the harp without hesitation. He couldn't explain it, but after the few exchanges he'd had with Eva he already trusted her more than her brother.

She tried first plucking, then tapping the longest string. It didn't work. Her rose-pink lips pursed in concentration as she tried again, tapping it harder. This time it rewarded her with a deep, resonating tone that carried over the water. Looking up at him, her eyes shone bright, her smile brighter. "'Tis quite difficult," she admitted cheerily.

"That's why they have you start training so young. But you could still learn to play with great skill, even beginning now."

"Thank you, Finn. Really," she choked out the word. "I'm embarrassed to admit how much I appreciate this. I've always wanted to learn to play."

"Try playing the same note, and pausing it with your other hand," he suggested, steering the conversation to safer ground. She'd never learn to play if neither one could focus on the task at hand.

She did as he said but struggled to pause the sound cleanly.

Without thinking, Finn placed his hand over hers, pressing it against the string with proper form. "Like this," he said softly, not sure why he felt the need to whisper.

"I should let you return," Eva replied, rising quickly and handing the harp back to him. "I've taken up so much of your time already, and you'll be spending all day teaching the men tomorrow."

"I'm teaching them poems," he reminded her, his voice still quiet, "not to play an instrument. It's no trouble at all, but if you're weary I'll walk you back." Against his better judgment, he offered her his free hand.

And she took it.

# CHAPTER NINE

EACH NIGHT AFTER dinner for nearly a fortnight, Eva met Finn by the water's edge and fumbled her way through his lessons. For days, it was the only thing she thought about, the only thing she looked forward to in her life. In the last few lessons, Eva finally convinced herself that Finn had meant it when he told her he wasn't teaching her out of pity. Aye, she'd even go so far as to call him a friend.

The thought brought a smile to her face and joy to her heart.

Fastening her cloak about her shoulders, Eva set out to check on the progress of the kitchens. After the fire, she had insisted that they be rebuilt in order to correct whatever oversight had caused them to malfunction. Illadan and Cormac both questioned the necessity of it, but Eva stood firm on being thorough. The last thing she needed was an accusation of treachery against the household of the king.

"How is the progress today, Tómma?" she asked the carpenter when she reached the kitchens. Looking about, it seemed to her they were nearly finished. She strolled carefully from one end of the large room to the other, eyeing every table, cupboard, and oven as she went.

"They'll be finished by morn," Tómma replied. "Your cook should be able to reclaim her kingdom in time to prepare tomorrow's meals."

Eva nodded, hiding the giddiness that overcame her at finally finishing the project. She couldn't wait to tell Finn—he'd listened to her every triumph and obstacle over the course of construction. He'd once jokingly suggested she compose a ballad about the ordeal.

Looking Tómma directly in the eyes, to ensure he wasn't lying, she asked the most important question. "And what has been done to prevent another fire, compared with the previous construction?"

Of course, she knew from the outset what his plan had been, but it would be remarkably irresponsible not to ensure he'd done as promised.

"Not a single item made of wood is within ten feet of any of the hearths or ovens, milady." He gestured toward the items as he spoke. "The tables and stools have been sealed with a wash of lime to help prevent them catching fire, should they be placed too close. And, most importantly, I've extended the channel running through the church all the way here, that there is a source of water within the kitchens should a small flame need dousing."

Eva moved around a large wooden table to have a better view of the floor at which he pointed. Though much of the floor was packed earth—without flammable rushes atop it—along the wall shared with the church a small row of stone flooring as wide as her arm lay, running the length of the wall. In the center, a deep groove carried water from a natural spring on the other side of the hill to a cistern large enough to hold the overflow. Eva had seen the design in monasteries first, to bring fresh water to their extensive gardens and their own kitchens. Once she learned of it, she wondered why anyone would do otherwise.

Nodding her approval and thanking Tómma for his fine skill and hard work, Eva took her leave to relay the good news to Illadan. He'd been pestering her for several days as to how much longer they'd be forced to endure the carpenter's ceaseless hammering and sawing. She knew that today, the day before the trials began, the three judges would likely be holed up in the solar discussing the particulars of the following day.

The buildings at Cenn Cora were almost all separate. Though

some, such as the kitchens and the church, shared a common wall, they had no door connecting them. Eva entered the royal family's quarters, where Illadan and Cormac lived and worked. Doors of carven oak opened into a small receiving room, lit by braziers and decorated with several chairs and one long bench. A single guard stood watch at the back of the windowless room.

"Illadan?" Eva queried.

The guard tilted his head in the direction of the solar.

Eva nodded her thanks and headed down the narrow corridor. She heard men's voices long before she reached the first door on the right. It was cracked just enough to betray their conversation. Eva had no intention of eavesdropping, but when she heard the topic of their conversation, something inside her bid her wait.

"...lurking around Finn's tent." It was Illadan speaking.

"Are you certain?" Broccan questioned. "You were drunk off your arse last night."

"I was not!"

Broccan laughed until Cormac's serious voice interrupted. "He's probably found a lady from the village is all," he suggested.

Eva's heart rose into her throat. What on earth were they talking about? Had they discovered her meetings with Finn by the lake?

"Then he needs to go to the village to see her," Illadan replied. "I don't want strange women wandering about the men's tents at night. 'Tis utterly undisciplined."

Pain gripped Eva's chest, followed by an unfamiliar feeling. Jealousy? Could that be it? She shook her head to clear it of such nonsense. Why should she care if Finn had taken a lover?

The thought brought another surge of jealousy, frustrating her further. It wasn't as though they were courting. Indeed, it wasn't as though they could *ever* court one another.

Oh, aye, Eva knew she felt a close bond forming with Finn. And the man was too charming for his own good. He seemed to always know what to say to coax a smile from her, no matter how forlorn she felt. Finn was always kind enough to go out of his way and cheer her up.

Which was precisely the problem. Finn was dangerous, Eva realized. She grew far too fond of him with each passing day. Particularly when considering the myriad barriers that would prevent them from ever becoming more than friends.

First, she had no interest in anything but service to her family. She had decided after losing her second betrothed that she would not marry, which is why she had been living happily in the monastery at Cill Dara until Sitric came for her that fateful night.

Second, as a hostage, she would have to convince Brian to allow her to marry—a formidable task, to say the least.

Third, Dallan would never approve the union, for so many reasons Eva didn't even bother contemplating them.

Finally, and most importantly, every single man in her life was either in constant danger or already dead, mainly due to her bloodthirsty cousin Baeth. She was not about to bring yet another sheep to the slaughter. Her position as a daughter in the house of one of Brian's greatest enemies meant any man tied to her was also tied to an early grave.

"We'll keep an eye out," Cormac's deep, even voice tempered her frantic thoughts. "I can ask around to ensure 'tis nothing nefarious. And we can remind the men that trysts should happen elsewhere."

For what seemed like the hundredth time in the space of a minute, Eva reminded herself that in spite of whatever ridiculous, inexplicable response she might have to the news that Finn had a lover, she was not—was *absolutely not*—jealous.

And for the hundredth time in the space of a minute, her heart ached.

# CHAPTER TEN

I T WAS GONE. His harp was gone.

Finn overturned the ten items he owned, all of which were too small to hide anything. He dismantled his pack. He even picked up the cot he slept on, though he couldn't imagine how it would have gotten under there.

*Of course*, he thought bitterly.

He was surrounded by the sons of wealthy lords, and some thief chose the only item of value he'd ever owned to steal. Righteous fury descended upon him, filling his lungs with fire and his mind with only one thought: he was going to get that harp back.

He'd come to his tent to get it for his lesson with Eva, but that would have to wait now. Instead of wandering down to the lakeshore, Finn stormed back up to the great hall. He didn't stop until he found Illadan, standing on the dais talking with Broccan.

Illadan's eyes widened when he spotted Finn striding toward them. Broccan frowned at him with concern.

"Finn," Illadan greeted him, his eyes wary. "What can I do for you?"

"Someone stole my harp."

"You're certain? 'Tis quite an accusation to throw around."

"Mayhap 'twas the woman you've been trysting with," Broccan grumbled, crossing his arms and widening his stance.

Finn's pulse raced. Did they mean Eva? Did they know he'd been meeting with her each night? Finn glared at him. "Excuse me?"

Illadan sighed heavily, shooting Broccan an exasperated glance. "We've spotted a woman sneaking around your tent of late," he explained. "It seems a good time to remind you to take your trysts outside of the encampment."

Finn took a full step backward, absorbing what seemed a ridiculous statement. "Had I a lover, my lord, I assure you I would do as you ask."

"Are you saying you didn't invite any women to your tent?" Broccan's skepticism fanned Finn's anger.

"I've just said as much, haven't I?" He grew weary of the ridiculous turn of this conversation. "I must recover my harp. I don't know who's taken it, but I assure you, it has nothing to do with any women I know of."

"Indeed." Illadan rubbed his chin thoughtfully. "I shall see what I can learn. Have no fear Finn Ulfsson, the bard shall have his harp."

"You have my thanks." Finn somehow managed a nod to Broccan before finally heading toward the lake to meet Eva. He'd packed her a rather large meal this time, which he meant to give her an earful over. She'd been eating just fine until tonight. For some reason, she'd not attended dinner.

As Finn wandered down the wooded path toward Loch Derg, an odd thought crossed his mind. Almost as ridiculous as the conversation he'd just had.

Eva hadn't been at dinner. A woman had been snooping around his tent. Now his harp was missing.

She couldn't have stolen it, could she? Finn could hardly believe he was thinking it, yet nagging doubt wouldn't relinquish its hold. Were Eva and Dallan using him for some greater plot he'd yet to uncover? He knew Dallan still kept secrets from him, but Finn had truly believed Eva to be trustworthy. Could he have misjudged her so gravely?

He shook his head, huffing at his own thoughts. Of course not. Eva would never do such a thing. Though he was terribly concerned over why she'd missed dinner. Was she ill? Dallan had hardly said a word the entire meal he was so concerned over his sister.

Finn's head swam with anxiety, frustration, and confusion as he walked. He had no idea what was going on, and even less of a plan for dealing with it. First, he was going to forget everything and try to enjoy some time with Eva. Hopefully he'd be able to sleep then, at least. He wasn't even going to think about the trial tomorrow.

After Finn learned that she couldn't swim, he'd made Eva promise never to come down to the shore alone. Their new arrangement was for her to wait for Finn on a large, smooth stone about halfway between the fortress and the lake.

She wasn't there.

Finn's heart hammered in his chest as he approached the clearing along the shore where they were to meet. Still no sign of Eva.

Had she been attacked? Had she fallen in and drowned? Gods, where was the woman!

He stepped onto the small beach, his answer awaiting him. When he saw Eva standing there, alone by the lake, breaking her promise plain as day, he opened his mouth to tell her exactly what he thought about that.

But then she turned around and all thought fled him.

There, clutched in her arms, was his harp.

# CHAPTER ELEVEN

*Earlier that day*

EVA PACED THE rush-covered floor of her chambers in exasperation. What on earth was the matter with her?

The thought of attending dinner, of seeing Finn now that she knew he had a secret lover, turned her stomach sour. Nay, she could hardly breathe, let alone eat. She couldn't possibly attend dinner. She wasn't ready to face him yet, and she knew he'd be looking for her come nightfall. He had no idea that anything had changed between them.

Eva groaned in frustration. It shouldn't matter at all to her. But it did.

He hadn't done anything wrong. She shouldn't be upset with him.

But she was.

Which is why, instead of attending dinner, Eva rushed down the trail toward Loch Derg in search of solitude and comfort, intending to be safely back in her quarters long before Finn came. As she raced toward the lakeshore, her tears began to fall. She was so overcome by her whirlwind of emotions that Eva didn't notice when she ran right past the stone where she had sworn to stop and wait for Finn.

She didn't realize she'd broken her promise to Finn until she barreled through the trees and onto the sandy shore.

To find that she wasn't the only one seeking the solace of the lake.

Eva halted instantly, regretting her recklessness.

A woman sat by the water's edge, her face turned away from Eva, her sand-colored hair reminiscent of Finn's. Eva began to tiptoe back into the cover of the trees until she noticed what the woman held in her lap.

Finn's harp.

Eva would recognize it anywhere. Why this woman had it, she couldn't imagine. But Eva knew Finn would be wanting it back. So instead of retreating, she advanced.

"I suppose you had to sneak into his tent to get that?" she asked, hoping this meant that Finn did not, in fact, have a lover.

The woman's head snapped around and Eva drew in a heavy breath. She knew she wasn't masking her shock well.

The woman, of an age with or perhaps younger than Eva, was so covered in bruises that her features were nearly impossible to discern. "Are you alright?" Without thinking, she rushed to the woman's side, hoping her injuries weren't as grave as they appeared.

Thief or not, no one deserved such treatment.

The woman burst into tears before Eva could get another word out. She reached a hand out in comfort, but the woman flinched away. Oh, aye, someone had hurt her terribly.

Eva swallowed, taking a deep breath and contemplating what to do next. She needed to get the harp, but this woman was clearly in very serious trouble and needed help. She'd need to tread carefully on both counts.

"I'd like to help you," Eva said softly, so as not to startle her further. "We should get you to a healer."

The woman shook her head. "I'm fine." She wiped the tears from her own cheeks, wincing when her hand pressed on the bruises. "I've been to one already."

So many bruises.

"Who did this to you?"

The woman sniffled. "It doesn't matter. It's done with now. I'm here for my brother."

"Who is your brother? I can fetch him."

"Oh, no!" The woman tried to stand but fell back down. "You mustn't! He can't know I'm here! He'll send me home."

Eva wasn't sure if that was a good thing or a bad thing, so she decided to humor the woman. It could very well be in her home that she'd received such abuse.

"I won't tell him," Eva assured her. "But I would still like to know who he is."

The woman looked down at the harp, then back up at Eva. "His name is Finn."

"Finn Ulfsson?" Every word out of this woman's mouth only shocked Eva further. Though, it did now make sense as to why the woman's hair reminded her of Finn's own.

Her face lit up. "You know him?"

"Aye, I know him," Eva replied, remembering the many times he'd spoken fondly of his younger sisters. "And I know he'd want to know about whatever trouble you're in. He cares deeply about his family. You're Ethlinn?"

She nodded. "He already knows." Ethlinn hung her head in her hands and started sobbing again. "This is all my fault!"

Something inside Eva snapped at that statement. "I don't know anything about what happened, but I can tell you with absolute certainty that *none* of it was your fault."

Ethlinn looked up at her through tear-stained eyes and smiled hollowly. "I wish that were true."

Eva smiled at her encouragingly. "If Finn knows you've been so badly treated, why is he here and not seeing to you?" She knew how Finn doted on his sister—all of his siblings, really. She couldn't understand why he'd abandon Ethlinn when she truly needed him.

Ethlinn tilted her head curiously. "Why do you think he's here? Naught can be done in this world without funds or connections. We have neither, so my foolish brother is risking his life for vengeance on my behalf. And I won't stand for it."

"What do you mean?" Eva knew Finn to be many things, but

foolish was not one of them.

"He's making a huge mistake," Ethlinn groaned. "He thinks he can somehow fix this, but he can't. I need to get him out of this contest before he gets himself killed. He's a bard, not a warrior."

Eva's heart went out to her. "Now *that*," she whispered, "is a sentiment I can understand."

"It is?"

"As it happens, I have my own foolish brother who, against my wishes, has also joined the trials."

"Really?" For the first time since they'd started speaking, Ethlinn sounded relaxed.

Eva nodded, but as she looked at the harp in Ethlinn's lap, she felt urgency return. Finn would be coming soon, and if Ethlinn wanted to continue hiding from him she'd need to be going.

But not before Eva got Finn's harp back.

"You know it's going to break your brother's heart when he realizes that's gone."

Ethlinn sighed. "I know," she admitted. "But it was the simplest way I could think to prevent him from competing in tomorrow's trial. If I can get him out of the contest before they start trying to stab each other, mayhap I can save his life and he'll come back home."

"Ethlinn," Eva hesitated, "I wish I weren't the one to dash your hopes, but Finn will pass the contest whether you take his harp or not. 'Tis poetry, not music. He won't need it."

The stricken look on Ethlinn's face shattered Eva's heart. "What? Is that true?"

"Believe me, I wouldn't have said so otherwise."

"Now what will I do?" Ethlinn tried to stand, once again falling back down.

Eva reached for Ethlinn's arm to help her, realizing too late that it was covered in bruises.

Ethlinn winced, grabbing Eva for support. As Eva helped her to her feet, she noticed that the poor woman was skin and bone.

"Have you eaten while you tracked your brother here?"

Ethlinn shook her head. "I foraged some tubers and wild garlic, but I haven't had the energy to do much else. Normally I would hunt, but I'm having trouble even drawing my bow."

"Here's what we're going to do," Eva commanded, leaving no room for argument. "You give me the harp and I will return it to your brother. First thing tomorrow morning, you will meet me here and I will bring you a proper meal and as much as I can find to tide you over on your journey home. In exchange, I won't say a word to Finn about any of this."

"I'm not leaving until I get Finn out of the trials."

Eva nodded. She could appreciate that sentiment. "Fine. But when you do, you'll travel with proper rations."

"He'll think you stole it, you know," Ethlinn remarked, handing the harp to Eva.

Eva shrugged. "I'll think of something."

Ethlinn looked as though she might hug Eva for a moment, but then her eyes went wide. "Someone's on the trail," she hissed.

"You go, I'll handle it."

Ethlinn squeezed Eva's arm, mouthed "Thank you," then disappeared into the woods far from the trail.

Just in time for Finn to emerge from the trees.

Eva heard Ethlinn let out a gasp, giving away her position nearby. Apparently, his sister hadn't gone far.

Finn strode toward Eva, fire in his gorgeous blue eyes as they took in first her, then his harp in her arms.

He stopped just before he ran into her, his voice a low growl. "I think we need to have a talk."

# CHAPTER TWELVE

"Eva," Finn began, his voice tight with anger, "why do you have my harp?"

Eva opened her mouth several times, like a salmon washed ashore. Her eyes darted to the tree line behind him, before returning to hold his gaze.

"Did you sneak into my tent?"

"I, um." Her eyes went to the tree line again.

Finn glanced behind him. Was she planning some sort of attack on him? What kept catching her eyes? He began scanning the trees himself, but she grabbed his shoulder and turned him to face her.

"I did not sneak into your tent," she answered at last. "And I did not steal your harp. Though," her voice faltered, "I can see where it might seem that way."

"Oh, can you now?" Finn crossed his arms but felt some of his anger abate. He wanted to believe her. "Then how is it you've come to be in possession of it?"

Eva rolled her lips together while she thought.

For the briefest moment, Finn wondered if they were as soft as they looked. Then he remembered that he was, in fact, furious with her.

"I, um, I was quite upset today," she began tentatively. Unconvincingly.

"About what?"

"I'd rather not say," she replied sharply.

Finn couldn't hide his amusement. "And how will I know you tell the truth if I don't know the whole of the story?"

"I doubt you'll believe it either way." The same fire he'd felt when he stormed onto the shore came to life in her emerald eyes.

"So far I have nothing to believe," he challenged.

"Fine!" She jabbed him in the chest with her forefinger. "You want to know why I was upset? I thought *you* had some secret lover sneaking into *your* tent at night that *you'd* never told me about." Every time she said "you" she jabbed him even harder.

Finn grabbed her finger before she got any more ideas, holding her warm hand in his own. She'd been jealous. And she'd not wanted to admit it.

He pulled her toward him, still holding her hand. *"You* broke *your* promise."

"I did." Her whispered admission fell across his face, filling him with her intoxicating scent.

He'd never been so close to her before. And though he knew he should drop her hand, create some distance between them, he couldn't back down.

"I found the harp by the water's edge, and I heard someone running off when I approached." Her eyes strayed once more to the tree line.

"Did you see them?" Finn ground out, his anger surprising himself. If he was to believe her tale, Eva had been here alone with the thief. Did she not see the danger in that?

She shook her head. "I'm sorry, Finn. I'm sorry I broke my promise."

"And…" he prompted.

"And what? I didn't steal your harp, truly."

"Perhaps not," he allowed, still uncertain as to whether he believed her, "but you *did* skip dinner."

She pulled herself up taller, throwing her shoulders back in her indignation. And inadvertently highlighting her heaving chest. He'd certainly managed to rile her, he thought, forcing his eyes back to her face. Reluctantly.

"I must apologize for skipping a meal?"

"Aye," he growled, "to your brother. He was beside himself with worry over you."

"I caused my brother to worry," Eva's low, throaty voice teased, "or you?"

Before he could think better of it, Finn captured her lips with his, overcome with an unquenchable desire to taste her.

She squealed and pushed him away. Hard. Then she tumbled backward, nearly losing her balance, her eyes shifting wildly toward the tree line.

Finn caught her but released her like a hot iron moments later. Because, apparently, he had horribly misread that situation.

A great, gaping hole of embarrassment opened in the center of his chest, and his only wish was that it would grow large enough for him to fall into and disappear. What had he been thinking? Of course, a *princess* wouldn't want to kiss him. By Odin, what a fool he was.

"I'm so sorry," he hurried to apologize, likely too little too late. "I don't know what came over me."

He knew exactly what came over him. What he didn't know was why he ever imagined Eva would reciprocate his desire.

Her cheeks flushed a deep, gorgeous rose.

He needed to get away from her before he said something even more foolish. Or, heaven forbid, *did* something even more foolish. Recognizing defeat, Finn hastened to extricate himself from this awkward situation, moving far too quickly toward the path up the hill.

"Finn!" Eva called as he disappeared into the trees. "Finn! Wait!"

But he couldn't. He'd never been so embarrassed in his life. When he heard her footsteps after him, he took off running and never looked back. Whatever she wanted to say would have to wait until he'd regained some small shred of dignity.

How could he have been so foolish? Even if she had wanted the kiss, there were a hundred reasons it was a terrible idea. He was here to help her escape to freedom, was he not? If he and Dallan succeeded, Eva would disappear once the trials ended.

Dallan. Finn sighed as he finally reached his tent. Dallan was the most important reason Finn could never, ever kiss Eva. He couldn't betray his closest friend by secretly seducing his sister.

Finn didn't stop until he was sitting on the cot in his tent, his head hanging between his hands as he relived that torturous moment repeatedly. He reached for his harp, as music always helped calm him, only to finally understand why Eva had been yelling at him to wait.

She still had his harp.

# CHAPTER THIRTEEN

FINN WOKE TO the sound of Dallan shouting at him, and for one horrifying moment he thought that Dallan knew he'd kissed Eva.

"It was an accident!" he shouted, half asleep, his mind a fog-covered field.

Dallan shook Finn's shoulder until he opened his eyes. "Get up!" he hollered, likely loud enough for every warrior in Cenn Cora to hear. "You'll miss the trial!"

That got his attention. Finn shot out of bed, pulling on his clothes and running out of the tent without a word to Dallan. He'd have to thank him later.

And not just because he felt guilty about kissing his best friend's sister. He doubted he'd ever stop feeling guilty about that.

ALL THE WARRIORS assembled in the courtyard outside the great hall. Illadan, Cormac, and Broccan stood in front of the towering double doors in nearly identical stances—arms crossed and faces serious. Finn searched the crowd for Eva, eventually spotting her face peeking out one of the windows of the great hall. She met his gaze, her rose-petal pink lips propelling his thoughts to kissing her. And to how horribly wrong that had gone. He looked away to spare her the trouble.

Illadan briefly addressed the men, explaining that he thought it a greater challenge to perform outdoors, where your voice could easily be carried away by a mischievous wind.

As Illadan's speech drew to a close, he signaled for the men to begin forming a half-circle around a stool nearby. Illadan, Cormac, and Broccan stood at the outermost edge of the ring of men.

As Finn and Dallan sat on the damp, dew-covered grass, Ardál made his way to join them. A lean warrior from a house of lesser kings, Ardál had been the only one other than Finn who knew all twelve books well enough to help teach them. He was a skilled poet and bard, capable and well-versed. Finn had set twenty of the men under his tutelage over the past two weeks. Both he and Ardál would be judged on the overall performance of the men they'd taught.

They hadn't a moment to speak before Illadan called the first of the men to perform. Finn's mind raced as he watched. They wouldn't be able to get through all the men in one day. Illadan had said on their first day at Cenn Cora that the trials would run for a fortnight, but he doubted they needed quite that long.

The first performance went adequately. The lad forgot several lines, but overall he had the verses well in hand. Illadan sounded distracted as he called up the next man. Out of the corner of his eye, Finn noticed that Illadan had slightly shifted his positioning. Instead of facing the man performing, he now had a clear view of the tree line on the near side of the fortress, where the path began that led down to Loch Derg.

As the first poem started up again, an uneasiness gripped Finn. Something felt off. He looked again at Illadan, which only unsettled him further.

The prince appeared utterly unaware of the trial going on before him. His stone-cold stare remained fixed on the forest. If looks could kill, those trees would be up in flame. Every so often, Illadan took a calculated step further around the circle of men, closer to the tree line.

Dallan nudged him, nodding toward Broccan.

Finn looked away from Illadan only to find that Broccan, too, had noticed Illadan's odd behavior.

As the performance neared its midpoint, Illadan casually walked over to Broccan, whispered something, then disappeared behind the great hall. Finn hardly heard the rest of the poems. One more man performed before Broccan called everyone to a midday meal in the hall and a brief reprieve from the increasingly repetitive trial.

The central hearth glowed in welcome, the tables already laden with crusty bread, smoked salmon, and buttered greens. A pleasant breeze poured in through the open windows. And Eva stood waiting, hands folded, worrying her lips.

Finn sucked in an anxious breath, fighting every urge to walk up to her and apologize yet again. He reminded himself she very well may have stolen his harp, and that he should absolutely not still be thinking about kissing her.

*If* one could even call that a kiss. He was fairly certain that when the lady shoved you aside quicker than you could draw breath it likely didn't count.

"What's wrong with Eva?" Dallan asked Finn under his breath as they took seats opposite one another. "First, she misses a meal, now she looks wracked with nerves. Did she say anything to you? Did you find her last night?"

Gods, he hadn't told Dallan anything yet. He'd gone to bed and come straight to the trials without uttering a word to his friend.

Finn cleared his throat, taking a swig of ale. What could he possibly say?

*Your sister thought I had a lover, skipped dinner out of jealousy, put herself in danger by running down to the lake alone, and possibly stole my harp. Also, I kissed her and she hated it. Sorry.*

"Finn?"

"I think she was anxious over your performance today," he lied. What an awful friend he was.

Dallan snorted. "Anxious I'll pass onto the next trial, more like."

Finn shrugged. He decided to keep his mouth shut before he made more a mess of things.

"So you found her then? Last night?" Dallan pressed. "Or is this pure conjecture?"

A timely commotion at the door came to Finn's unlikely rescue. Illadan burst in, looking less composed than Finn had ever seen, reminding Finn of an angry bear.

"Finn Ulfsson! Outside! Now!" Illadan let the doors slam hard as he strode back into the courtyard.

Perhaps it hadn't been a rescue after all.

"We can talk about it later," Finn promised Dallan as he stood to follow Illadan. When he passed through the threshold to the courtyard, he heard fifty men rush to stand beside the windows.

But Illadan was nearly across the courtyard already, heading for the family quarters. "Solar!" he shouted without looking behind him.

Moments later, Finn entered the small solar and Illadan slammed the door shut behind him.

Illadan rounded on him with terrifying intensity. "Are you aware that your sister has been beaten to the point of being unrecognizable?"

Finn hadn't known what to expect, but certainly he hadn't thought his sister would be the issue. Ignoring his confusion, he answered honestly. "Aye," he spoke carefully. "It happened some weeks ago now."

"And are you also aware that she is starving near to death in the woods surrounding Cenn Cora?"

Finn's head spun. "What?" He couldn't comprehend it. "She's here?"

"You didn't invite her, then?"

Without asking, Finn fell into the nearest chair in shock. "I must see her home," he muttered, still having difficulty believing Ethlinn had been so foolish as that. "You're certain it's my sister? Ethlinn?"

"As of right now I am certain of very little," Illadan replied tersely. "But I am certain it's your sister."

"Please," Finn could hardly get the words out, "please let me feed her and take her home."

"Is it safe for her to return?" Illadan asked. "Or will she be subjected to the same treatment?"

"Our home is safe," Finn assured him. "She must stay away from the *crannóg*."

Illadan looked fit to murder the next man to cross him. "Who lives in the *crannóg*?" Rage dripped from each of his words like a violent promise.

Finn watched Illadan uncomfortably. Why would he want to know? "My lord," Finn began slowly, carefully, "I appreciate your concern for my sister, but I assure you…"

"Who?" he shouted impatiently.

Finn sat back in the chair. He had never seen Illadan in such a state. Likely his sister had done something to prick the prince's temper.

"Ernin mac Shay," Finn answered. "He's a lesser king over the lands we call home."

Illadan began pacing, rubbing his chin thoughtfully. "What's the nearest town?"

"His *crannóg* is on a small lake north of the village of Ath Dara."

"Thank you."

Illadan's dismissive tone concerned Finn. He stood from the chair to block Illadan's exit. "You never answered my question," Finn reminded him. "May I have your leave to take my sister safely home?"

"No." The prince reached around Finn for the doorknob. "Any who wish to join the Fianna may not leave this area during the trials. I will take her."

"Am I not permitted to speak with her myself?" Finn couldn't hide his exasperation at Illadan's vague, irrational responses.

Finally, Illadan looked at him with some semblance of compassion. He put a heavy hand on Finn's shoulder. "'Tis for the best you do not, I think. She came here to undermine you, to keep you from succeeding in the trials."

Now *that* sounded like Ethlinn. Finn was no longer surprised at Illadan's uncontrolled rage. Though he desperately wished to argue, he nodded his understanding instead.

He followed Illadan in silence back out to the courtyard where all the men had gathered to wait for the trials to resume.

"Broccan, Cormac," Illadan called, "I need to speak with you. Men, take a break. Trials will resume in the morn."

A murmur of confusion rolled through the assembled crowd. Men wandered back to the encampment. Finn searched the tree line for signs of his sister. When his gaze fell upon a woman near the trail down to Loch Derg, his chest rose. But it wasn't Ethlinn.

It was Eva.

She motioned for him to follow before disappearing into the woods.

"What was that about?"

Finn hadn't seen Dallan walk over. "Your sister wants to meet with me."

"No, not Eva," Dallan said dismissively. "What did Illadan want?"

"Tonight, I will explain everything," Finn promised. His friend deserved the truth. Except maybe the part about kissing his sister. "But your sister is down at the water waiting. It must be important."

Dallan finally understood. He glanced at the forest, then back at Finn. "You'd best go."

Indeed. Finn hurried after Eva, deciding precisely what he would say when he finally caught up to her. He didn't know what his sister plotted. He didn't know what had happened with his harp and how it had ended up with Eva. He certainly didn't know what to make of Eva's odd behavior. But Finn knew one thing for certain.

He owed Eva an apology.

# CHAPTER FOURTEEN

EVA PACED IN frustration in front of the large meeting stone. She had to tell Finn about Ethlinn.

While all the men waited in the hall and the courtyard, Eva had managed to slip around to the back side of the royal quarters, beneath the windows of the solar. She heard the entire conversation.

And she knew that Finn was likely equal parts worried about, and infuriated with, his sister. Though she doubted he'd disobey Illadan's orders, Eva felt compelled to speak up on behalf of Ethlinn, as Finn had been doing for her with Dallan.

When Finn finally appeared on the path behind her, Eva's pulse quickened. Heat rose from her belly to her cheeks as she remembered the end of their conversation last night. Lord, he'd actually kissed her.

The look on his face when she pushed him away had split her heart in two. She'd hurt him.

He thought she didn't want him to kiss her, that she didn't care for him.

Though, if she were honest, 'twas probably better to let him think that.

To admit the truth of it, to acknowledge how much she'd wanted that kiss, would only create more trouble. There was no space in her life for romance. Even if, by some miracle, Brian and her brother and Sitric all agreed to allow her to marry as a hostage, Eva would refuse it. Every man she'd ever loved had died because of Baeth. And Finn, as a warrior of the Fianna, would be in danger for much of his life. Even now, the thought of losing him tore at her. And Eva knew 'twould only worsen.

Finn halted two arm's lengths away from her. "Eva," he began.

She held up her hand to silence him. "Before you say anything, there's something I must tell you. I spoke with Ethlinn yesterday. And this morning as well."

Finn's gaze hardened, his eyes a dark, dangerous sapphire. "Why did you not tell me?"

"She asked me not to."

Eva knew the moment he put it all together.

"Ethlinn stole the harp," Finn guessed.

"She did." Eva took several steps toward him. He felt too far away. "Because she worries for you, as any sister ought."

Finn stood silent, motionless for several torturous moments. "You let me believe you a thief to protect my sister."

Eva felt her blush return as he drew closer. Her mind strayed back to the previous night. To how close they had been before he kissed her.

"Yet you also allowed her to stay, knowing her intentions of interfering in the trials."

"She made a good point. One I myself had wondered over many times."

"Please," his husky voice sent a tingle down her spine, "enlighten me."

"You trained as a bard, not a warrior," Eva explained softly.

Finn's jawline tightened noticeably. "I told you already—"

"I know," she interrupted. "I know. But hearing it from your sister gave me greater cause for concern."

"Just because I can sing, you believe I cannot fight?" he challenged. "I assure you, my lady, I am quite physically capable."

All the air left her lungs in one great rush. She should tell him why she couldn't let him kiss her last night. She should leave before she said anything more at all. She should return to her quarters before she gave him a false sense of hope. Instead, she did the most unreasonable thing imaginable.

She kissed him.

Or tried to do. As it turned out, 'twas not so easy a task to kiss a man twice your height without involving him in your plan. As she stood there on her tiptoes, thinking he'd meet her halfway, he looked confused.

He leaned down but didn't touch her. "I thought," he whispered, "last night…"

"Last night I wanted you to kiss me. I didn't want Ethlinn to see it." Eva wished it weren't true. Everything would be far simpler if she felt nothing for Finn. But, though her mind knew naught could happen between them, her traitorous heart refused to listen.

Before she could gain control of herself, his mouth covered hers, capturing her next breath and robbing her of all sense.

Other than that unfortunate occurrence the night prior, Eva had never kissed anyone before. Her heart pounded painfully against her chest as his lips claimed hers.

His hand went to the small of her back, pressing her so close to him that she could feel every hard inch of him against her. He certainly wasn't lying about being physically fit. His tongue teased at her bottom lip, igniting a fire inside her like she'd never felt before.

Finn surrounded her; he was the entirety of her world in that moment. The warmth of his body against hers. His intoxicating scent of earth and spices. His honey-sweet taste on her lips. The sound of his labored breathing as he devoured her.

It felt so right to be in his arms.

Without warning, he pulled back. "Eva."

The hitch in his voice only fanned the flame now burning within her. "Finn? Why…"

"We can't," he breathed, "I can't." He dropped his hands from her like he'd been burned. "I don't think we should meet here again."

The flames sputtered out, replaced by an ache centered on her chest. "You mean to kiss?"

"I mean at all. Eva this cannot be. And I cannot trust myself to be alone with you any longer."

Tears threatened, but Eva managed to hold them in. "And if I need to send a message to my brother?"

Finn's smoldering eyes raked over her. "Then wear the cream colored gown."

She let the first tear fall as she watched him walk away. Knowing he was right did naught to ease her sorrow.

⤜⤛⤜⤛

HE WAS GOING straight to Hell, as his mother liked to say when she was unhappy with his behavior. Dallan had asked him to cheer up his sister, to keep her company, to take her messages. Not to kiss her senseless.

The memory of her lips drove him to distraction as he made his way back to his tent. He could still feel the shape of her against his hands, could still hear the soft, delicious noises she made.

He could still see the hurt on her face when he told her they couldn't meet any longer. But a daughter of kings deserved better than the son of an Ostman farmer. And his friend deserved better than betrayal.

Dallan spotted Finn the moment he entered the encampment. "Now will you *please* tell me what is going on with Illadan? What did he need to see you about?"

"It seems my sister tracked us here from the *crannóg*." Finn kept his voice low, not wanting to start folk talking.

"Alone?" Dallan's chestnut eyes went wide. "Through the wilderness?"

Finn nodded.

"Is she alright? Where is she?"

"Illadan found her today," he explained. "That's why he ran off, he spotted her in the trees. She needs nourishment but is unharmed. Illadan is taking her back to my parents."

Dallan looked askance. "Illadan? But what about the trials? He's the leader of the whole contest."

"I know," Finn shrugged. "I told him I would take her, but he said none of us could leave during the trials."

"They let us go to the village," Dallan mumbled. "I don't remember them ever saying we couldn't leave."

Finn thought back to Illadan's fury. "He didn't seem himself. I'm not sure what happened when he met my sister, but it upset him deeply."

"But it's all taken care of?" Dallan's voice held nothing but genuine concern for his friend. "She'll be alright?"

"Of course," he assured himself as much as Dallan. "Illadan is a strong, capable leader. I'm sure he has everything well in hand. What I wonder is if they'll need to find a third judge."

"So what did Eva want?" Dallan asked as they reached Finn's tent. "It must have been pressing to meet in the middle of the day."

Finn ran a hand through his hair. "She had heard about my sister. She had much the same questions as you."

Dallan nodded. "She must have heard Illadan speak of it with the others."

"Precisely."

Guilt wracked Finn as he stepped inside his tent. He really was a terrible friend.

# CHAPTER FIFTEEN

THREE WEEKS. FOR three long, arduous weeks, Finn had done his utmost to avoid her. The first few days, Eva thought that perhaps he would relent. Of course, he felt badly about kissing her—Dallan was his friend. Eva could understand that. Surely, he'd come around once he realized 'twas a harmless kiss. It wasn't as though she was looking to marry.

When it was clear he meant to avoid her, Eva got angry. How dare he? Woo her, kiss her, then push her aside like scraps from his supper? Here she'd thought he was honorable, but this was unconscionable. Brother's friend or not, had he not considered *her* feelings? Oh, aye, if he'd thought to speak to her then, she'd have had a thing or two to say. And he wouldn't have liked any of it.

She'd simmered like that for nearly an entire sennight, glaring at him through much of dinner and grumbling the few times he'd come within earshot. But a few days ago, she decided that she wasn't some helpless damsel. She wasn't going to just wait around for Finn to change his mind—as 'twas clear he would be doing no such thing. Nay, she'd take charge and *make* him notice her again.

While she couldn't wear the cream gown until she truly had something of merit to say to him, lest she risk angering him, Eva could certainly draw attention to herself. She had several ideas, but what she really needed was advice. She'd never *actually* tried to get a man's attention before.

So, one morning before the men were set to practice for the second trial, Eva cornered Cormac in the hall as he broke his fast. She'd have preferred Illadan, as he was so easy to speak with and she knew him better, but Cormac would have to do. No one else dared to be caught speaking alone with a hostage save the two princes. She walked purposefully to his table, rehearsing in her mind the conversation she'd planned all night.

"Eva," he greeted her warmly, "what a pleasant surprise. Please, join me."

She sat down across from him, pouring herself a cup of water and gathering her strength.

Cormac eyed her suspiciously. "Was there something you wished to speak of?"

There was nothing for it. She dove in headfirst. "I overheard my maids speaking of matters that are...unfamiliar. To me. I had hoped you could perhaps offer some insight."

Cormac's face paled. He looked horrified.

Eva pressed her lips together to suppress a laugh at his reaction. "They were discussing things that men admire in women, but it seemed their list required the man to already be well acquainted with the woman in question."

"I see," he replied slowly, taking a deep drink from his own cup. "And how may I be of help?"

"I must imagine that there are certain qualities that a man would notice about a woman when he first meets her. As I am not a man, nor familiar with any, I couldn't imagine what those might be. I had hoped you could enlighten me."

Cormac stared at her for several moments, clearly contemplating her bold request. "You wish to know what I notice during my first conversation with a lady?"

Eva nodded. "Yes. In particular, what you might admire about her that you would want to become better acquainted."

When he hesitated, she continued. "'Tis only for my own edification, to sate my curiosity. I assure you I have no intention of courting or marrying." She felt a twinge of guilt at misleading him, but she wasn't lying entirely. She had no desire whatsoever to marry.

She *did* want to kiss Finn again, and she'd determined that staying away from him was more harmful to her than kissing him while knowing he could never be hers.

Cormac cleared his throat, looked around the room, then leaned across the table toward her. "Very well," he agreed quietly. "I cannot speak for other men, but I find my own eyes drawn to a lady's hair first."

"You mean the way it is braided?"

He shook his head. "The way it moves and shimmers, like waves in the sea. I know 'tis the style to wear it up and braided, but men notice it far more when it flows freely."

"Fascinating." Now *that* was something she could use. "Anything else?"

"Next would probably be the color of her eyes or the readiness of her smile."

Hmm. She supposed she could smile more, but 'twas naught she could do about her eyes.

"And of course," he continued, growing more comfortable with her questioning, "there's the way she carries herself."

Eva leaned forward. "How do you mean?"

"Does she walk with confidence and grace, as a woman who is certain of herself and her own abilities? As I said, though, those are but my thoughts. I cannot speak for all men."

Even so, he'd given her quite enough to get started.

Eva thanked him and excused herself, heading to her quarters to prepare. Though she had occasionally peeked out to watch the men train, she had mostly made herself scarce and kept busy around the keep. Now that the kitchen was finished and she'd adjusted to her daily duties, Eva found herself with more time alone than she wanted. Especially without her evenings spent in Finn's company, it grew more difficult to keep herself from falling back into the darker turns of her lonely mind.

Which was precisely why she needed to convince Finn to

stop avoiding her. Though she had greatly enjoyed kissing him, more than anything she missed his company.

It took her quite a while to unbraid and comb her hair so that it laid nicely down her back. She hoped Cormac would politely ignore the fact that she clearly was acting on his insights from that morning.

Grabbing an empty basket, Eva strode out into the sunshine-filled courtyard. The men were already training in the field just outside the keep's walls. She could hear the sounds of weaponry in use and a good deal of shouting as well. A light breeze played with her skirts and tugged at her unbound hair. The morning sun warmed her cheeks as it peeked out from behind a fluffy white cloud.

Entering the field, she pretended not to notice the men there, practicing with spears and shields. Instead, she walked slowly and confidently around the edge of the field, well out of their way, and began picking the yellow gorse flowers that had just started coming into full bloom. After several minutes of determinedly ignoring the men, she casually looked in their direction.

Only to find that she could not look away.

Finn, like many of the other men, had removed his léine. Wasn't that considered sinful? She'd seen men working their fields do so in the heat of summer, but even that was rare. More often than not they'd roll up their sleeves or pant legs and carry on.

Yet here they were, a dozen or more men without a stitch of clothing on their upper half. And the presence of a woman appeared to have no effect whatsoever on their senses of modesty.

She spotted Finn instantly. He was easily the tallest of the men, and one of the broadest as well. In fact, she hadn't noticed until now just how large he was in comparison with the other men. The muscles in his shoulders and arms rippled as she watched him raise his shield to block a spear. She suddenly wished she'd brought along a waterskin, for her mouth had gone terribly dry.

Eva watched his entire sparring match, ignoring the tightening in her belly every time Finn's muscles moved. His motions held an ease that belied the hours he had likely trained to defend himself so capably. His strength, his agility, his masculine beauty took her by surprise, captivating her.

As his bout ended, his eyes caught hers. She'd been staring, and he'd noticed.

Eva averted her gaze as quickly as she could, but she knew he'd seen her looking. For all she knew, her mouth had been open as a trout's as well. She'd come here to capture *his* attention, not divert her own.

Not wanting to appear *too* guilty at being caught gawking, Eva resumed her flower picking, glancing toward the men every so often to see if she'd finally gotten him to watch her. She stayed with the men for several hours, until she had to go oversee the preparation of the midday meal.

Not once did Finn spare her a glance.

# CHAPTER SIXTEEN

"SOMETHING'S WRONG WITH Eva." Dallan voiced Finn's own thought aloud as they finished up their morning defense training. "She wasn't out this morning."

Finn nodded his agreement but kept his own counsel. "Perhaps they needed her in the keep," he offered, trying to ease Dallan's mind though he didn't believe it himself. In the weeks they'd spent together, Finn realized that Dallan's concern for his sister occupied much of his time that was not devoted to training—a fact that compelled Finn to keep his own suspicions regarding her behavior from Dallan.

In truth, Finn was relieved when Eva didn't come to watch them train that morn. Oh, aye, he was no fool. She was playing some sort of game with him, but he wasn't going to play along. Of course, he'd noticed that she wore her hair down now. How could he not?

Every time he saw her, beautiful silken waves the color of willow bark fell across her back to her tempting hips. She walked circles about them in the field, picking flowers and casting him sidelong glances. The first day she'd been out he even caught her staring at him. Hopefully her brother hadn't noticed as well.

She came out each morn for three days to torment him, making him work twice as hard to ignore the beautiful temptress while he trained. Today she hadn't come.

Normally, he would have thought as he told Dallan, that some other task required her attentions. Except he had also noticed a change come over her at dinner each night.

Instead of glaring at him, she looked absently over the room. She smiled less each day. And last night, she hadn't eaten any of her meal, putting Finn in mind of the first time he'd noticed her lack of appetite. Aye, Finn feared that Dallan's observation was correct: Something was wrong with Eva.

Dallan sighed, his thoughts clearly still on his sister. "Would you meet with her again? For me?" he whispered, handing a shield to Finn to stack with the others. "I know you said she wanted to take a break from her lessons, but she seemed so much happier then. Could you just check on her? Maybe you can convince her to take up playing again."

Finn's conscience warred within him. He wanted to help his friend. He wanted to help Eva. Yet he still didn't trust himself to see her alone. When he was with her, all logic fled in the face of his need to hold her. Neither the knowledge that one of them would be leaving, or that he was sneaking around behind Dallan's back, could break the enchantment she had on him. Even now, he struggled to keep his thoughts off her; 'twas only a matter of time before he struggled to keep his hands off her as well.

"Please, Finn," Dallan pleaded. "At least meet with her and ask her."

"I'll go speak with her this afternoon," Finn agreed reluctantly. "But I don't know about the lessons."

"Ostman!"

Finn and Dallan both turned to see Diarmid approaching with two shields. He tossed another one to Finn to stack up. Diarmid, along with his brother Conan, had been placed in charge of training the men for their defense trial. Over the past sennight, Finn had come to know both men well.

Conan and Diarmid were the younger brothers of Cormac, and therefore distant kin of Brian and the princes of Connachta. Distant enough, Dallan had explained, for their sister, Dunla, to have married the aged king. All three brothers shared dark hair and strong, pleasing features, but the similarities ended there.

Cormac, from what Finn could gather, was quiet and contemplative. He seemed to bear the heavy weight of familial responsibility almost entirely on his own.

Diarmid, the youngest, had an infectious thirst for life and could charm the skirts off an abbess. Conan had the heart of a warrior and the bravery to go with it. He was kind and funny and could best most anyone in a drinking contest, but he was not so wild as Diarmid.

"Are you ready for the trial?" Diarmid asked, stacking the other shield himself. "Only a few more days of training."

"I was ready a fortnight ago," Dallan boasted, walking to fetch a stray spear.

Diarmid chuckled and folded his arms across his chest. "Oh, aye? So that's why you were falling over your own feet a sennight ago?"

Dallan's face reddened. "Once! I tripped once!"

"Once that we saw," Finn added, nodding conspiratorially to Diarmid.

"Traitor," Dallan grumbled.

"What about you, Ostman?" Diarmid asked Finn as they all turned together to walk to the hall. "Will you pass the trial?"

Finn grinned at him. "If I don't, I'd better be in Valhalla," he replied. When Diarmid had first called him Ostman, he'd been furious. But it had since become something of an endearment and a joke.

"If they'll take you," Dallan teased. "You go to church an awful lot for a pagan. I could see where there might be confusion."

"Tell me you lot aren't *joking* about the defense trial." Conan, the middle O'Conor brother, frowned at them like an angry nursemaid. "You do realize men are going to die, don't you?"

"In my experience, the best time to indulge a sense of humor is right before the possibility of death." Diarmid delivered this wisdom with his widest, toothiest grin.

Conan shook his head at his younger brother, instead turning to Finn and Dallan. "I think the pair of you will live," he told them. "Whether you pass or not is another matter."

Dallan immediately took exception to that. Finn, however much he believed in his own abilities, acknowledged the truth in Conan's statement. To pass the test of defense, one did not simply need to survive. One needed to survive uninjured. A single, glancing scrape from a spear and all chance at success was lost.

Eleven men had failed the test of intelligence, incapable of adequately performing the twelve books of poetry. Forty-two warriors would compete in the next trial, and Finn feared that Conan was right: some would likely die. Apart from the test of bravery, defense was the most dangerous trial.

When they reached the great hall, Finn, Dallan, Conan, and Diarmid sat together at a table near the great open hearth in the center of the room. As a matter of habit, Finn glanced at the spot where Eva normally took her meals. She wasn't there.

Unease coursed through him as he recalled the last time she'd missed a meal, going down to the water alone in spite of her promise. Finn knew she didn't take his concerns seriously, but he had seen men who knew how to swim drown. He had no doubt she'd be in real danger if she fell into the lake she loved so much.

Panic descended as he searched the tables in earnest, hoping she'd simply chosen to sit elsewhere. Finally, just as he was about to excuse himself and go search for the daft woman, he found her.

Along the edge of the room, sets of chairs and benches had been positioned to create areas suitable for private conversation. Of course, in a room so frequented as the hall, truly private conversations did not exist. A handful of alcoves offered the most privacy, though they still sat in plain view of anyone in the room paying attention.

Tucked away in one of the alcoves on the far right side of the room, Eva sat working on something in her lap. Finn couldn't quite make it out, what with half a dozen tables and twice as many men between them, but he thought it might be mending or sewing.

She looked up from her work briefly, but long enough for Finn to see what she tried to hide, to see what Finn had tried to ignore.

He'd been avoiding her out of loyalty to Dallan and out of fear of his own weakness. He'd seen all the signs, watched her eat less and less each day. Watched her disappear slowly, fading in body and spirit to meld into the shadows. For the past three weeks, Eva's melancholy crept bit-by-bit back into her life. He could see in her absent, wandering gaze that she was as lonely now as she had been when first they met.

Only this time, he knew what to do about it.

# CHAPTER SEVENTEEN

HE WAITED UNTIL most of the men had left to take a short break before he approached Eva's alcove. Dallan nodded his thanks as Finn turned toward Eva.

As he drew nearer, Finn saw that she worked on embroidery.

"What are you making?" he asked, sitting down on the other chair in the alcove.

She didn't look up from her work as she answered. "A baby gown for Astrid."

"Your cousin? Yes?"

She nodded.

"Is she expecting a child soon?" Eva had spoken much of her cousin, Sitric's younger sister, but Finn couldn't recall her ever mentioning a husband or children.

"No," Eva replied softly.

"Is she hoping to have a child soon?" Finn wasn't going to stop until she spoke more than a single word in response. "Perhaps she's gotten betrothed?"

Eva finally set down her work in a huff and looked up at him.

A small victory. He knew he had a long way to go, however. She wouldn't easily forgive his treatment of her these past weeks.

"I simply wish to know why you're making it for her," Finn explained gently. "'Tis all."

Eva's face fell from defiance into sadness. "Because I miss her," she whispered. "And I know she's eager to start her family, whenever Sitric finally finds her a husband."

Finn's heart ached for her. He couldn't imagine being separated from all those you loved, even the ones living right beside you. "Have you heard any news of her?"

She shook her head, picking her embroidery back up to resume her work.

Well, he had his answer. Eva was most certainly not alright. And he wouldn't leave until he'd cheered her at least a touch. He decided to change to a lighter topic.

"What about you?" he asked.

"What about me?"

"Are you eager to start a family?"

A bitter laugh escaped her lips. "Not in the least."

How had they never discussed this? "Why not?"

"Why should I be?" she countered. "Why would I want to bring some poor man into a family constantly at war? Why would I want to risk my life birthing a son only to lose him in a battle twelve years later? To have him murdered by a cousin who wishes no competition for the throne? To lose a daughter in childbirth at sixteen?"

"Twelve is a touch young," Finn offered, "but I see your meaning."

"Brian's brother died at twelve."

"So, your plan is to never love anyone ever again so that you don't have to suffer through losing them?" This had not been the cheerful conversation he'd hoped for, but he knew it was an important one, nonetheless.

"My plan is to stop selfishly endangering others just so that I feel loved."

"Everyone needs to feel loved," Finn reasoned. "'Tis not selfish. 'Tis necessary. The people we love and who love us, they are what make life worthwhile. *And,*" he added emphatically, "not one of those deaths would be on your conscience. No one has died because they loved you."

"The two men I was to marry did. My father did."

Finn couldn't hide his shock. "You were betrothed?" he said, louder than he'd intended. "Twice?"

"Years ago, when I first came of marriageable age." She set down her embroidery again. "My father arranged a match for me with a lord's son, Duncan. He kindly exchanged several letters with me, and I fancied myself in love."

A pang of jealousy shot through Finn as he listened to her speak of this other man.

"My father insisted on finding a man near my age, at least, after what happened with my aunt. While we were still planning the wedding, war broke out. My second cousin, Baeth, made a grab for the throne, dividing our family. Duncan fought with my family to prove his loyalty to our kin, to me. He was killed, and I was devastated."

"Eva," Finn kept his voice low, steady, "you must know he was duty-bound to stand with your kin. I'm certain he cared for you, but he would have fought whether he did or not."

"And what of the man that Baeth assassinated shortly after our betrothal? Who's to say he wouldn't come after the next man I tried to marry?"

Finn ran a hand through his hair. Anyone would be melancholic with a family like that. The worst part is that whoever married into Eva's family would never take the throne. That poor bastard had been killed out of sheer spite. "Should you ever wish to marry, I will kill your cousin myself should you desire it. Then you shan't have to worry."

She smiled sadly. "Don't make promises you can't keep, Finn."

Here was his chance. He feigned affront at her statement. "You think I couldn't defeat him?"

Finally, she laughed. A single, small chuckle slipped out and warmed Finn's heart.

"Can I ask you something personal?" She sounded hesitant for the first time since they'd started talking. "What happened to your sister?"

"Our local lord desired her," he could barely speak the words.

"She resisted."

Eva gasped, a look of horror on her face. "No," she breathed. "How awful! Finn, I'm so sorry. Did the lord pay your family the fine?"

Finn swallowed his anger, taking several deep breaths. Just thinking about what happened to Ethlinn made him question his decision to *not* attack the bastard right back. But Ethlinn and his mother had begged Finn and his father to wait for justice. Only justice never came. And his family didn't have the funds to pursue further retribution.

He shook his head once.

They sat in silence a long while, Eva quietly embroidering and Finn contemplating his next course of action. He hadn't realized how much he'd missed Eva, how much he enjoyed sharing these moments with her, even the serious ones.

"Do you still wish to play the harp?" he asked at last.

The smallest gleam shone in her emerald eyes. "Do you still wish to teach me?"

"I thought, perhaps, we could meet here after dinner each night and play for an hour or two. Surely the household will appreciate the entertainment. They've been after me for weeks to play more often."

"Yes, but 'tis my poor playing they'll endure," she giggled. "Not your incomparable talent."

"Your skill grows each time you play," he assured her. "They'll love it."

And so would Finn.

# CHAPTER EIGHTEEN

S HE HAD GONE fully mad. Eva paced her chamber for what seemed like the hundredth time since she met Finn. Pacing had become her new pastime, it would seem. Wringing her hands, she questioned yet again the decision she'd already made. Perhaps she was setting herself up for another disaster.

Her lessons with Finn went better each evening. The first night after they'd resumed her instruction had been uncomfortable at best. She was so used to being alone with him on the beach that an audience made it difficult for her to play. Finn assured her it was even better to learn this way. After all, one performed music in front of an audience. Better to get over her nerves now instead of facing them the first time she played in public.

After two more lessons, it felt as though they'd never been apart. Eva could barely contain her excitement each morn enough to make it through to the end of her day for her time with Finn. It terrified her just how much happier she felt when he was a part of her life. She couldn't imagine how awful it would be without him.

Which is precisely what prompted her plan.

Tomorrow Finn and Dallan would both compete in the trial of defense, which consisted of nine men throwing spears at them. Her hands shook just thinking about the danger they'd be in, and how little she could do to help them. Either one could be killed tomorrow. She still had no interest in marrying, or even seriously courting, Finn, but she'd be damned if she didn't get one last kiss from him.

Eva determined that she needed to meet with Finn alone tonight. Hopefully, he cooperated. Smoothing out her cream dress for the hundredth time since she'd donned it, Eva worked up the courage to finally go to the hall for dinner.

"I can't believe how well she plays," Dallan's voice swelled with pride at his sister's accomplishment. "She took lessons for years. I don't know what you're doing differently, but it's working."

Finn feared that falling in love with his student was what he was doing differently. Of course, he'd never admit that to Dallan. Or Eva. After hearing her thoughts on love and marriage, that seemed a poor idea.

"I can't believe Cormac let you sit so near to her," Finn changed the subject.

Dallan grinned. "I'm winning him over. Though I doubt he'll let me speak to her, at least I can be present in her life."

They sat at their usual table, finally able to eat after a hard afternoon of training. Eva had yet to appear, and Finn couldn't stop himself from checking her table between each bite of his meal.

"Ostman!" Diarmid and Conan sat down next to them, one on each side of the table.

"Were you trying to kill us this afternoon?" Dallan asked, shoving a large bite of roast boar into his mouth.

"If it will keep you from dying tomorrow, I will push you today," Conan replied evenly, not the least concerned over the brutal practice they'd just finished.

"I don't hear the Ostman complaining," Diarmid baited Dallan. "Isn't that right, Finn?"

But Finn couldn't respond. Eva had finally appeared.

Wearing the cream gown.

"Finn?"

Why was she wearing the cream gown?

"Finn!"

"Sorry." He somehow managed to take his eyes off her, which momentarily halted his highly inappropriate thoughts about a certain woman taking off a certain cream gown, and his growing concern over *why* she wore it. "I was thinking about tomorrow." Nope. Not even a little bit.

Nine men throwing spears at him could not possibly be more of a challenge than getting through dinner and *not* sprinting down to the lakeshore. Yet, somehow, he managed it. He pretended to listen to his friends' lively discussion. He acted like he wasn't having trouble keeping his eyes off Eva. And at the end of the evening he walked, looking calm and composed, toward the forest path when inside his mind raced and his heart pounded.

Why did she want to meet with him? Was something wrong? Did she want him to kiss her again?

That thought halted him under the thick canopy of trees. Gods, what if that's what she wanted? Would he do it again? At this point, would it matter?

Fighting hard to push such thoughts to the back of his mind, Finn continued down the forest path toward the stone where he knew she waited. More than likely, she was simply worried over tomorrow's trial. Aye, that was it.

"I was wondering if you'd come." Her breathy voice made every part of his body tighten.

He offered her his hand, helping her up off the stone. It was so small inside his own, so delicate. "Curiosity got the better of me, it would seem."

They walked hand-in-hand until they stood before the rushing water. The wind howled across the valley, whipping the surface of the lake into a frenzy of white-capped waves, storming the sandy shore like an invading army.

Finn felt Eva shiver, her hand wiggling in his. "Where's your cloak?" he asked, unfastening his own and draping it over her shaking shoulders.

"I didn't expect it to be so cold."

"It's after dark."

"'Tis nearly midsummer, though."

As much as he loved debating Eva, Finn didn't want her out here too long, even with his cloak on her.

"Here," he ordered, tugging her hand and guiding her under the shelter of a towering pine. He sat down, leaning against the trunk. "Now, what is it that is so important that you'll risk freezing to death?"

She shot him a skeptical look and sat down entirely too close. "Isn't that a bit dramatic?" When he didn't answer, she continued. "I wanted to ask you two favors and send a message to my brother. I also wished to speak to you without the entire household listening."

Reasonable enough. "The first favor?" he prompted.

"Before I ask it, I feel that it's important for me to tell you how worried I am over tomorrow's trial. You could be killed."

"'Tis true," he allowed, "but unlikely. 'Tis more likely I would be wounded and survive."

"Finn," her voiced faltered, "I would really miss you."

"What are you asking me, Eva?"

"I want you to kiss me again, and not get cross with me this time."

"I wasn't cross with you," Finn told her. "I was angry with myself for betraying your brother's trust. He sent me to watch over you and instead I took advantage of you."

Eva pushed up onto her knees, so close that her leg brushed Finn's and sent a burning sensation straight through him. "You didn't take advantage of me," she corrected him, her voice husky. "I asked you to kiss me. And I'm doing it again. Let me worry over my brother."

Against his better judgment, Finn cupped the back of her head, pulling her lips onto his in a searing kiss. The last time he had been gentle, in case it was her first. This time he let his passion run wild. He didn't just want to taste her. He wanted to devour her.

His tongue parted her lips. His hands ran through that hair she'd been tempting him with for more days than he could track. She melted into his kiss, her body contouring perfectly to his own, but he needed more.

Slowly, so that she could stop him if she wished it, Finn's hands dropped from her hair to her hips. All he could imagine was holding those hips tight while he thrust himself deep inside her. He squeezed them, catching her gasp with his mouth before his lips carved a sensuous path down her jaw to her neck.

"Do you want me to stop?" he heard his own ragged voice, hardly able to believe he managed the question.

"No," she replied firmly. "I want more."

Good. So did he.

He picked her up and set her in his lap facing him, so that her legs went to either side of him. Gods, she weighed less than those damned shields he was tossing around all day.

Her hands went straight to his chest, her eyes clearly trying to see straight through his shirt.

He let out a rough laugh. "I saw you watching me."

"You had your shirt off." Her fingertips brushed his collarbone seductively. "I didn't have a choice."

He captured her mouth again, taking her over and over as he grew so hard he thought he might explode. His hands swept up from her hips, spanning her waist briefly before he brought them to rest over her chest. She moaned as he began massaging her, letting his hands explore the fullness of her perfect breasts.

The longer he caressed her, the longer he kissed her, the more difficult the thought of stopping became. He knew 'twas now or never, and though he apparently no longer had problems kissing Eva, he was most certainly not going to bed her.

Keeping her in his lap, his hands about her waist, hers rubbing his arms, he pulled his lips away and smiled at her.

"Thank you," she whispered, her forehead leaning against his, their noses touching.

"My pleasure," he replied honestly, wondering how long they could sit this way before his desire got the better of him. "What was your second favor?"

"Tomorrow, after the trial, there will be a feast. A celebration for those who succeed at such a difficult test of skill. I want you to dance with me."

Finn brought his hands to her cheeks, holding her face tenderly as he gave her the answer she wouldn't like. "I can't. I'm sorry."

Her face fell. "You can kiss me like that, but you can't dance with me?"

"Dancing is public. That kiss was *very* private."

Eva thought that over. "True. But people dance together all the time. And you tutor me already in public. No one would think it odd."

"If I put my hands on you to dance, everyone would know that we do far more than play harp together."

"Why? What do you mean?"

Finn sighed. "Eva, every time I touch you, every time I'm this close to you, it's all I can do not to throw you onto the ground and show you far more than a simple kiss. Trust me, no matter how hard I try, I won't be able to hide how badly I want you."

"Well," she breathed, "that certainly is the most flattering way to refuse a lady."

"'Tis the truth. Otherwise, I wouldn't refuse you."

Eva shivered again and Finn hugged her against him, kissing her hair and inhaling deeply. "You need to get back inside," he chided. "What message shall I give Dallan?"

She pulled back to look at him, her eyes twinkling with mischief.

"Is he going to punch me when I relay this message?"

"Probably not," she replied seriously. "Tell him I wish him well in the trial, and I hope a spear catches his arm."

"You can't be serious."

"If he's injured, he won't be able to continue with his misguided efforts at heroism. I don't need saving. He does. And that spear is my best bet, assuming it doesn't kill him."

"Very well," Finn conceded, helping Eva to stand and guiding her toward the path. "Let us depart so I can relay your well wishes for your brother."

Halfway up the path, where they normally part ways so as not to be seen walking out of the forest together, Eva turned to Finn one last time. Even in the shredded moonlight, Finn knew her face had gone pale.

"Please be careful tomorrow," she said softly. "I can't lose you, too."

# CHAPTER NINETEEN

THE MORNING OF the trial, Eva walked with every member of the household to the practice field to watch the event. She had hardly slept the night before, between remembering Finn's kiss and worrying over him and her brother. The hilltop buzzed with wagers as to who would pass this difficult and dangerous test of skill.

For her part, Eva estimated that this trial would reduce the number of competitors by half or more. Even if men weren't killed, she knew the likelihood of injury was great, and not everyone was skilled with a shield no matter how hard or long they practiced.

The clear, bright morning, crisp but warm, stood in stark contrast to the seriousness of the day. Eva sat beside her maids at the front of the crowd. Most folk brought woolen blankets to cover the damp ground beneath them, but Eva and the other ranking nobles in the keep had stools carried out to sit upon.

The look of the field sent chills down Eva's spine. Even as a means to test a warrior's skill, this particular challenge had an air of the morbid to it. Each of the forty-two remaining men had dug a hole as deep as their waists. The men were tested three-at-a-time. Though their numbers were such that they could accommodate four, three was chosen as it is a sacred number in the hopes of bringing luck to the men.

The first group of three men jumped into the holes they had dug. The rest of the men quickly buried them in, so that they could only move from the waist up.

So that they couldn't move out of the way of the spears.

The only way to survive was to use the shield and staff each man held to deflect the spears.

Three groups, each with nine men, armed themselves with spears and counted out five paces—near enough to make a good, accurate throw without being too close. As the spear-throwers formed a line and raised their weapons, Eva sent a silent prayer of thanks that Finn wasn't in the first group of defenders.

On Broccan's signal, one after another down the line they cast their spears, waiting the space of a breath between each throw. 'Twas absolute chaos.

The sounds of shouting, cheering, and splintering wood assaulted her ears in a cacophonous roar.

At first, Eva tried to watch all three men defend themselves. Her eyes followed the first spears thrown at each, but by the time she'd looked back to the first defender, she started missing many of the throws. The entire ordeal was over in a matter of minutes—so much quicker than she'd expected.

It had taken weeks of training and a morning of digging for their fates to be determined in mere moments.

When the last spears had been thrown, the men rushed forward to help the defenders out of their holes and to check them for wounds. The first man had been cut on his arm. The third had a gash on his side. The man in the center wasn't moving. A spear had struck him straight in the chest.

All three of the first men had been eliminated from the trials, and one of them had lost his life.

What would happen if no one passed? Eva wondered if Brian had planned for such a possibility.

A heavy silence descended over the spectators.

Cormac and Broccan rushed to the side of the man who'd been killed, but Eva couldn't see what was happening. All she saw was the man surrounded by as many warriors as could fit near him. After what felt an eternity, four men carried the fallen warrior toward the church. The two wounded men walked to the infirmary. And the next three men took their positions, buried to their waists, shields in hand.

Eva could barely bring herself to watch the next round. Luckily, no one died this time. Two men managed to come out unscathed, in fact. One man failed, but his wounds were mild.

As the third group of men took position, Eva's breath faltered. Finn and Dallan each dropped into a hole, taking hold of shield and staff, both their countenances focused and deadly.

She couldn't possibly watch both the entire time. Long before she felt ready, the spears started flying.

Her eyes flitted like a bird from her brother to Finn and back.

Finn caught the first spear on his shield with a thunderous crack.

Her brother remained unharmed.

Finn caught the second spear on his shield, alongside the first. The audience roared.

Dallan was still unharmed, three spears in.

Eva missed the third and fourth throws at Finn while she tried to determine how many Dallan had passed. She hadn't a moment to recover before two more spears sailed, one after the other, toward Finn.

He deflected both with ease. Eva let out a breath she hadn't realized she held, watching both her brother and Finn perform better than any other man she'd seen yet. Finn nearly took a scratch to the arm but managed to use his staff just in time.

Finn and Dallan had lived.

Eva barely saw the rest of the trial. Relief flooded her. Finn had lived. She hadn't realized just how worried she'd been until it ended. Now that it was over, a hundred thoughts rushed through her mind all at once.

Though grateful that her brother was safe, Eva had not been jesting when she'd hoped he wouldn't pass the trial. Getting away with a scratch on your arm, or even a small wound, was far better than bartering away your life in her estimation. Eva had been counting on him leaving after this trial. Now she didn't know what to do.

She'd clearly misjudged Finn. He had just proven that, bard or not, he was one of the most skilled warriors here. After that display, she wouldn't be at all surprised if he did make it to the end of the trials. She also thought, perhaps, he really could protect her from her cutthroat family. Mayhap he could even survive the many battles that would no doubt find her throughout her life.

Aye, if Eva ever decided such a risk to be worthwhile, Finn might actually be capable of surviving being betrothed to her.

# CHAPTER TWENTY

FINN COULD FIND no words to express his depth of feeling following the defense trial. He lived. And he had passed, as had the men he now called friends: Dallan, Ardál, Conan, and Diarmid.

Four men died. Their bodies were already on their way to families, that they might be properly mourned. Fourteen more failed for allowing themselves to be wounded.

After two trials, only two dozen men remained.

By midday, the trial concluded. Cormac decreed the next four hours spent in silence—one hour for each of the four fallen men. During that time, the kitchens worked nonstop to prepare a celebratory feast for that night.

Finn spent his time sitting on the hilltop, overlooking the blanket of forest and the gleaming lake that sat at its base. Dallan sat to his left, Diarmid and Cormac to his right.

They were the lucky ones.


"SO, IT SHOULD be easy after this, right?" Dallan handed Finn an ale, a triumphant grin on his face.

Finn took it from him, but before he could answer, Diarmid came over to join them.

"I wager you'll somehow manage to kill yourself running through the woods," Diarmid offered helpfully.

"Which time?" Dallan narrowed his eyes, as though it were a serious debate and not an utter farce. "When I'm being chased or pulling thorns from my foot?"

"Thorns, definitely," Finn declared. "It'll be the thorn that gets you."

"What are you ladies talking about?" Conan asked, walking over beside his brother.

"How I'm going to die," Dallan replied.

"What have we got so far?"

"Death by thorn whilst running in the woods," Diarmid told him, "but I think he may actually just trip and fall."

Finn took a swig of ale, letting himself enjoy a hard-earned moment of peace amongst friends. After the feast in the hall, the celebration had moved to the hilltop just outside the walls of the keep. Bonfires blazed, creating pockets of flickering light that illuminated much of the area. Of course, there were still shadows for folks who wished more privacy. The villagers from the settlement at the base of the hill had all been invited to share in the festivities, though Finn guessed in part it was to get more women attending as dance partners.

Tables with food and barrels of wine and ale sat waiting for guests. A fiddler and bodhrán player had come from the village. The steady drumbeat lent order to the wandering fiddle, delighting guests with lively, lilting melodies suited for dancing. The center of the field had become a sea of movement—swirling colorful skirts, ribbons, and flowers spun round and round as the dancers laughed and clapped.

A pang of regret struck Finn as he watched them. Lord, how he wanted to dance with Eva. He hadn't seen her since they moved out to the field, though she'd certainly been at dinner. Wearing the cream dress again.

Forget a thorn, that woman was going to be what killed him. Did she not know how she tormented him?

"Do you dance, Ostman?" Diarmid asked.

Finn turned to him, pulling his gaze away from the revelry before him. "No."

Dallan and Conan both looked at him with a mixture of horror and disbelief.

"Surely you must," Conan challenged. "Everyone dances, and you clearly have a love of music."

Conan sounded like Ethlinn. How many times had she said the same? Finn rounded on him. "I don't like to dance and I'm not particularly gifted at it, either."

Dallan smacked him on the back. "I do believe one may beget the other there, my friend."

Finn grimaced. "Not all of us were *trained* to dance as part of our education. I had more important matters to tend to."

"Like learning to play the harp and recite poetry?" Dallan countered. "Yes, I see where your rough upbringing in the back country wouldn't allow for such noble endeavors as dancing."

"Like tending the fields and minding the stable, more like," Finn replied. Dallan wasn't wrong, but Finn truly had never enjoyed dancing. He'd always preferred to play the music.

For Eva, though, he would have made an exception.

"Those village lads seem to be doing just fine," Diarmid nodded toward the dancers.

Finn glanced casually in their direction, contemplating his next defense, when the flash of a cream gown in the firelight caught his eye.

Eva stood in the glow of one of the bonfires, halfway around the field from Finn. Her hair fell about her shoulders. A smile brighter than the fires lit her beautiful face. Just seeing her warmed Finn's heart; her smile made it all the better.

Finn's enjoyment proved short-lived, however.

Some tall, confident, golden-haired farmhand strolled over to Eva, making a show of bowing and offering his hand. He didn't truly believe she would…

Gods, she was off to dance with the fool.

"Saints, Finn, we were only teasing."

"What?" Finn looked back to his companions. He didn't even know who'd spoken. All he knew was that Eva danced, this very moment, with some other man.

His attention returned to the field, where she twirled and laughed as the man swung her about. In the cream dress.

"You look ready to charge to battle." Dallan chuckled, stepping in front of Finn to demand his attention.

And block his view of Eva.

Finn stepped to the right so that he could keep one eye on the bold fellow.

"Maybe he's upset so many folk actually enjoy dancing," Diarmid prodded far too happily.

But Dallan knew Finn. His gaze followed Finn's to the center of the field, where Eva spun round and round, laughing. He raised a questioning eyebrow at Finn, crossing his arms over his chest. "My sister troubles you?"

Finn froze. That was a dangerous question. "Doesn't it bother you, her dancing with a strange man? Who knows what he may attempt?" He considered sprinting to the field to shove the bastard out of the way. Why hadn't he just agreed to dance with her?

"Clearly, it bothers you," Dallan observed. "Have a dance with her yourself if you're worried. You're big enough to scare the fellow off."

"I thought it would be inappropriate," Finn replied through gritted teeth, unable to look away from Eva, "seeing as she is your sister." Why did he feel as though he ought to punch the lad?

"God's bones, Finn! You're my friend," Dallan said incredulously. "By all means, rescue her! 'Tis not as though Cormac or Broccan will let me anywhere near her."

At that very moment, the farmhand in question slipped his hands over her hips.

And Finn lost all control of his actions. He let loose a choice expletive, eliciting an amused chuckle from Diarmid, before striding straight to Eva and that fool hanging off of her. He stepped so close they had to stop dancing lest they run into him. The sound of his three friends' laughter reached him all the way across the field.

Finn said nothing, glaring daggers at the man as he reached to pull Eva into his arms.

"Thank you for the dance, Simon," she called while Finn spun her as far away as he could get in one turn.

"A lady should know better," Finn growled, unable to keep his temper in check. His friends had been correct in their assessment. He *felt* ready to go into battle.

"Than to dance at a dance?"

"Than to dance with a strange man, who clearly had other intentions."

Eva twirled and grinned at him wickedly, the temptress. "I do believe the man I now dance with has other intentions as well."

"You'd better not have done that to trick me into dancing," he grumbled, nearly stepping on her foot when the tempo changed unexpectedly.

"It worked faster than I expected." She slowed her movements, allowing him to get his feet correct. "You could have just told me you didn't know how to dance."

"I could have," he agreed, "but it wasn't why I refused your request. What I told you was the truth."

His eyes fell to her bust. He corrected himself, but not before she noticed. In the soft orange glow of the fires, he could still see a touch of pink bloom on her cheeks. Gods, he wanted to kiss her.

"You're looking at me differently," she whispered. "What are you thinking about?"

He leaned as close as he could without being inappropriate. "Taking that gown off you," he whispered back.

For a moment she said nothing, and he feared he'd gone too far. He was about to apologize, when she finally spoke up.

"I'll be waiting by the lake."

The reel came to a spiraling stop and Eva, without so much as a backward glance, disappeared into the crowd in the direction of the forest path.

Finn cursed his own weakness, knowing he could only follow her.

Perhaps Eva wasn't the one who needed rescuing.

# CHAPTER TWENTY-ONE

EVA HAD FINALLY reached the end of her grand plan. She stood waiting by the stone, basking in her victory. She'd gotten Finn to dance with her, and she'd worn the gown so that she could spend more time with him. And maybe steal another kiss.

Alright, *definitely* steal another kiss.

A shiver of excitement ran down her spine as she thought about their last kiss. Surely there was no harm in kissing, right? Plenty of women kissed men and didn't marry them. She even knew a few who'd had babes with men and not married them. The church had several things to say about that, but most people went by the Brehon law, the laws that had been laid down generations ago, laws made by the ancestors of the lands in order to protect future generations. Even the local priests knew it, and many were supportive of the old ways of doing things.

So, really, there was nothing wrong with enjoying her kisses with Finn.

Unless Finn thought she intended to court him.

Eva swallowed hard. She absolutely couldn't marry him, which meant she had no business courting him.

The sound of footsteps coming down the path set butterflies off in her stomach, a regular occurrence when Finn appeared.

Lord, but he was handsome. He walked to her and offered her his arm without a word. His eyes were sapphires in firelight, burning the same bright blue as the hottest flames.

When they reached the lakeshore, he pulled her into his arms.

"You have to stop wearing that dress," he whispered, his hot breath sending shivers down her back. He leaned forward, their faces touching.

"I don't know why I would," she replied. "It seems to be working."

He grinned, his dimple sending a wave of tightness to her belly. "What exactly is it you want?"

Eva's heart raced in anticipation. "Another kiss."

His lips took hers, crashing against her as waves upon the shoreline.

It felt so good to be in his arms again. The world disappeared around them as Eva sank deeper into his embrace. She met his kiss, opening up to him in a way she never imagined possible.

His arms tightened around her, guiding her to lay on the sandy shore, his body covering hers in hardness and heat.

The scent of pine and *him* surrounded her, a delicious smell she couldn't define but that melted her every time he came near.

Finn's lips left hers, instead winding a searing path down her jaw to her neck. She couldn't believe how good it felt to be in his arms. Or that she had ever decided she didn't want this in her life.

As he continued to her shoulder, his hands ran from her hips to her chest. Slowly. Far too slowly. Eva arched her back, encouraging him to continue his exploration. Finn slid the neck of her dress over her shoulder, exposing her breasts.

His mouth covered her nipple, creating an uncomfortable ache between her legs. Eva gasped at the sensations in every part of her body. She felt Finn smile as he continued sucking and teasing her. Oh, yes, she'd made the right decision to keep kissing him.

His hand left her breast, gliding down her body to the hem of her skirt and then back up her leg. She should be scandalized. She should stop him.

But curiosity and desire won out.

And something else, something that went beyond the over-whelming urge to be closer to Finn, tugged at the corners of her mind. But in her haze of passion, Eva couldn't put a name to it.

All thought fled when Finn's fingers brushed her, sending tingles of pleasure through her. She wanted more.

Finn gave it to her.

His fingers slipped inside of her. First one, then another. Eva moaned, rocking her hips as he drove her mad. A pressure built inside of her, slowly at first, but as he continued Eva thought she might explode.

Did she need to do something? The sensation grew unbearable. "Finn," she gasped, finding it difficult to speak.

He leaned into her neck, nibbling her ear. "Let go," he whispered. His husky voice only propelled her faster toward wherever she was headed.

"Please," she begged, not knowing what she wanted.

His thumb rubbed in circles then, as his fingers continued moving in and out of her, and the world *did* explode then. Everything went dark, and for several breaths Eva felt nothing at all. When she opened her eyes, Finn smiled down at her.

Eva took several long moments to weigh what had just happened, collecting thoughts and questions.

"Is that," she paused, considering her phrasing. "Is that how you would conceive a child?"

Finn's eyes glinted in amusement. "Not exactly."

Eva nodded, contemplating. Finn lay beside her, and she felt the hard length of him pressed on her thigh.

"Can I do the same thing to you?"

This time he hesitated. "Yes, but—"

"Yes will suffice," she teased. "Unless you don't want me to."

"I do, but—"

Eva turned onto her side, reaching for the waist of his trews and giving him her most mischievous look. She didn't allow him to explain, taking him into her hand and testing different movements. When she ran a single finger along the smooth skin, he sighed, biting his lower lip in what was quite possibly the most attractive look she'd seen yet.

When she ran her whole hand down with a firm grip, he groaned. Heat flared once again in Eva's belly. She loved the way he sounded. Her hand kept moving, much like he had done for her, over and over until he let go a breath, his arms grabbing her waist, his seed spilling on the forest floor between them.

After cleaning themselves and readjusting clothing, Finn collapsed against the tree. Eva fell right beside him, her head resting on his chest. She could hear his heartbeat, could feel the rise and fall of every breath.

Perhaps she shouldn't altogether rule out a courtship. Or at least taking a lover.

If she was never to marry, what harm was there in enjoying her time with Finn?

"Eva," he broke the silence, his voice gentle, "I don't know if I can keep meeting with you knowing you don't want to marry." He looked at her, smiling despite the serious conversation. "I fear I'm growing rather attached."

She sighed. She'd known this conversation was coming, of course, but it didn't make it any less uncomfortable.

"I'm beginning to think taking a lover might not be so bad," she replied, letting her hand run over his chest. "I'm still not sure about marriage."

"Because of your family?"

Eva nodded against his chest. "But I am growing quite fond of you as well," she admitted, "and it's making me consider things I had already ruled out."

"I'll take what I can get, as long as I'm with you."

Eva couldn't believe how lucky she was to find such an understanding, kind-hearted man. Who also happened to be incredibly handsome.

She would think more on marriage, but for the moment she saw no harm in simply spending time with him. She might not intend to marry him, but that didn't mean she couldn't enjoy kissing him.

And maybe a little more.

# CHAPTER TWENTY-TWO

ONE AND A half full turnings of the moon later, a visitor arrived from Caiseal. Murrough, Brian's eldest son, pulled his horse to a clattering halt just as the noonday meal began.

Eva's mind fluttered far afield as she absently bit into an oat-cake. Since her tryst with Finn, she'd been able to think of little else. She desperately wanted to keep meeting with him in secret, to keep exploring the wild new feelings he stirred within her. They had both agreed to meet only in the hall for lessons, and to venture down for more intimate meetings only every sennight or so. She understood why they must not rush down that particular path, tempting though it may be.

When the doors opened and Murrough entered, a cold wave of foreboding smacked Eva's cheek. He could simply be visiting out of curiosity, to see how the trials progressed.

But something in her gut told her that was not the sole purpose of his visit. Caiseal lay two days' ride to the southeast, and Murrough was not a man at his leisure. He had a family of his own, duties to his king, and countless councils and errands to attend. Nay, Eva wagered he wouldn't be taking a trip only for the pleasure of it.

Dallan caught her eyes from across the room, his gaze filled with the same concern.

Something was afoot.

Broccan and Cormac rose to greet their esteemed guest. Eva stood and bowed as he passed her table.

And the rest of the meal, Eva pondered how she might discover the true purpose of his visit to Cenn Cora.

"YOU'RE NOT FOCUSING," Finn gently reminded Eva for the hundredth time that evening. "We can wait and practice tomorrow instead, if you'd like a night off."

The clatter of dishes and the shuffling of feet over dried rushes sounded behind them as the servants cleared the last remnants of the evening meal.

Finn and Eva had tucked themselves away in one of the alcoves, which afforded some privacy without being scandalous. Though, after what he'd done with her two nights ago, Finn felt like being in her presence was scandal enough. It certainly drove his thoughts that direction.

Eva waved her hand dismissively. "No, I want to play." The words tumbled out in a rush. "I'm terribly sorry for being difficult this evening."

"Difficult is convincing eight-year-old boys to sit still long enough to learn," he replied, thinking back to his own tutelage. "This is pleasant."

Her smile brightened even the darkest corner of the alcove. Gods how he loved her smile.

"How is your training progressing?" she asked. "I always thought the trial of movement would be the most difficult."

"More difficult than blocking spears and fighting a losing battle?" he replied skeptically.

She tilted her head, considering. "Mayhap not more than the spears," she allowed. "Fighting a losing battle is about overcoming your fear, which I think I could do. But movement," she blew out a breath, "well I doubt any amount of training could render me physically capable of jumping over a tree."

Finn laughed. "It's not a very big tree, if that helps."

"It's as big as you are!" she protested.

"Aye, but yours wouldn't be. It would only be as big as you."

"How would you even begin to manage such a thing?"

He had to roll his lips to keep from laughing at her incredulity. Her skeptical eyes were wide as the full moon. "You start by jumping over the tallest thing you can manage, then keep increasing the height."

"Well I, for one, can hardly wait to see this trial. I doubt anyone will be killed, and it promises to be a spectacular exhibition of skill," she declared.

Finn knew better. "You're thinking Dallan will never be able to manage it," he guessed.

"Of course! I've never seen him do anything of the sort. I'll be surprised if *anyone* can do it."

He decided it best not to mention that both he and Dallan had already managed it several times. "We'll just have to see, I guess," he replied, unable to keep from grinning.

"It'll be the opposite of the last trial," she predicted.

Finn could only nod in agreement. Though he doubted so many men would fail as she insinuated, he knew it would be more difficult than the test of speed. Almost a month ago, the men ran through the woods at a breakneck pace to outrun one another. Breaking a branch, tripping, or getting caught all resulted in elimination. Of two dozen men, only two had failed. It had been rather a pleasant trial, if grueling.

Diarmid and Conan both lost a wager that Dallan would trip over his own feet.

She pulled his harp closer, positioning her hands in preparation for playing. "What next?" she asked, looking up at him with mischief in her eyes.

"Why don't we work on a new piece," Finn suggested. That might help her focus better. "What would you like to learn?"

"Will you teach me the story of the salmon of wisdom?"

"Aye." Finn knew the tale well. His own parents had named him after the leader of the ancient Fianna, Finn mac Cumhail.

He'd grown up with his mother telling tales of their adventures by the fireside.

He placed his hands over hers to show her the first few chords, his palms burning like a bed of coals where they touched her.

She must have felt similarly, for she inhaled sharply as skin brushed skin.

The moment her green eyes caught his, Finn knew her thoughts had wandered to the same place as his own—a lakeshore at night, illuminated by the moon. Her body pressed against his. His hands exploring every delicious inch of her.

Finn swallowed hard, licking his suddenly-dry lips. "You'll want to start like this," he explained, silently congratulating himself on managing that much while his thoughts spiraled out of control.

After hammering out a few chords, he pulled himself together and they continued the lesson just like they always did. For all Eva gushed at Finn's talent, she herself had fair skill at the harp. Once she'd learned to play some of the more basic chords with proper technique, Finn found she had a soulful touch that made the harp sing. Her music ran deep. If she had studied alongside him as a youth, Finn wagered she might have surpassed him by now.

As it was, she'd made leaps of progress in her playing since that first lesson three months ago. At the end of their lesson that evening, Eva played the first two lines of the song flawlessly, the resonating notes echoing around the cavernous hall.

A single round of applause echoed from the doorway, startling both Finn and Eva.

Cormac walked over, his face unreadable. "Well played, Lady Eva," he remarked. "You are a credit to your tutor."

Eva and Finn stood together, as was polite in the company of a higher-ranking noble.

"Thank you, my lord," Eva answered quietly.

"I'm afraid I need to steal you away," Cormac kept his voice low, looking toward Eva. "We have a few matters to discuss that require your assistance."

"Of course." Eva replied, turning to Finn.

Finn knew the moment she let down her guard. When Cormac had appeared, all expression had left her face. But as she turned away from him and looked back to Finn, he saw the soft look in her eyes, the reluctant smile that told him she didn't want to leave. A swell of warmth rose in his chest at her intimate gaze. He gave her a reassuring grin and a gentle farewell before watching her walk out the door with Cormac.

The evening still young, Finn headed back to his tent in the fading sunlight. The entire world glowed the faintest, magical gold. When he got to his tent, he found Dallan alone at a campfire, staring into the flames pensively.

"Thinking of jumping in?" Finn quipped, taking a seat opposite his friend on one of the logs laid around the fire.

"Just watching them dance," Dallan answered, his voice distant. When he finally looked up at Finn, he didn't attempt to mask his surprise. "You're back early. Is Eva alright?"

Finn nodded, poking the fire with a stick. Not because it needed freshening, but because it was fun to play with fire. "Cormac needed to speak with her about something." When he saw the concern on Dallan's face, he quickly added, "He didn't look upset. I wouldn't worry."

"How is she doing?" Dallan asked, as he did every night when Finn returned from the hall. Some nights he came to listen to her play, but lately he had been leaving after dinner to train harder.

"She's learning a new song, the tale of the salmon of wisdom. She played the first chords flawlessly just before Cormac interrupted her."

Dallan smiled, sitting taller. "She's always loved music. I'm glad she's finally getting proper instruction."

"She's quite skilled," Finn agreed. "The music cheers her as well. I think she enjoys having company, but you've seen her face when she plays. I know that feeling, like there's nothing in existence except you and the music. It feeds your soul."

A shadow overtook Dallan's face, his eyes serious. "You think that even if she didn't have us with her, it would be enough?"

Dallan was in a state tonight. What had come over him, Finn couldn't say. Perhaps it had something to do with the secret Finn knew he still kept. He'd been training hard, pushing himself harder than any of the other men. And now he sat in deep introspection before the fire. Something clearly troubled him, and Finn sensed his answer held weight.

"I do," he told Dallan firmly, feeling the truth in it. "Even if she were lonely, the music would help."

Dallan nodded, his shoulders swaying slightly along with his head. "I'm going to need your help tomorrow, then."

"Of course," Finn replied without hesitation. "What for?"

"We're going shopping," Dallan's voice rang with determination. "I'm getting Eva a harp so she can play on her own and practice more. I'll be needing an expert's opinion when I commission it."

Finn stood, dropping the stick into the fire and watching it burn. "We'll go during the midday meal," he declared, heading to his tent.

Though he didn't relish the thought of visiting town, Finn could already see the look on Eva's face when Dallan gave her such a grand gift.

And, more than anything, Finn loved to see her smile.

# CHAPTER TWENTY-THREE

CURIOSITY PLAYED HAVOC with Eva's nerves as she followed Cormac through the quiet courtyard to the solar. She turned around to watch Finn leave the hall and head down the hillside. The grin he shot her made her cheeks warm and her belly flutter.

For a long time she had believed that Finn only taught her the harp out of pity, that their lessons were no more than a farce orchestrated by her over-protective brother. But as they spent more time together each night, Eva realized that Finn did seem to actually enjoy her company. And that was before they became more intimate. Entering the solar right behind Cormac, Eva couldn't help but feel grateful for Finn's friendship.

An aging fire crackled in a central hearth, the hot coals popping and hissing, the last licks of flame offering dim light to the room. Murrough sat in one of the chairs surrounding the hearth, his boots propped along the edge to warm them.

Cormac crossed the room, closing an open window. He gestured for Eva to join them in one of the chairs alongside the fire. As she settled her skirts, he finally began his explanation.

"Eva, you remember Murrough, Brian's son. He's come with a message from Brian regarding the end of the trials."

Eva nodded, furrowing her brows. "What do I have to do with the trials?" Thus far she'd been more or less excluded from anything to do with the trials themselves. Her focus was managing the keep.

"The trial of bravery has been revised," Cormac replied carefully. "We will now be traveling to Caiseal instead of hosting it here."

"Why?" The question was out before Eva could think better of prying. A wave of concern flowed from her chest to her belly. Would Finn and Dallan be in even greater danger? The test of bravery was the most difficult by far, and Eva knew many men would die for it.

Cormac looked to Murrough.

"It's best for as few to know as possible," the king's son answered. "We'll need you to help prepare the household for the move, to ensure we have enough servants and proper rations, things such as those."

"Of course," Eva agreed quietly, her mind racing as it took in this new turn of events.

"Wonderful," Cormac declared. "We'll be leaving the day after the trial of recovery concludes."

"Will I travel with you?" Eva asked.

Cormac shook his head. "You'll stay and await our return. Whoever makes the journey back to Cenn Cora will be the new Fianna. While you're here, you should have everything prepared to host a great feast in honor of those men."

A jolt of anxiety shot through Eva. Her brother and Finn would be performing the most difficult trial away from her. Were they marching to battle? Were they entertaining the king's court? What if something happened to one of them and they never returned?

"Allow me to escort you back to your quarters," Cormac offered, standing and walking over to Eva.

"Thank you." The whispered words held a hollowness she felt to her very core. Whatever the king was now planning, Eva knew it would be dangerous.

They walked in uncomfortable silence all the way to Eva's door. Cormac put a hand on it, looking around the courtyard.

"I would ask that you not mention this change in plans to any of the men," he said in a low voice. "I know you've a great fondness for Finn, but all the men must have the same amount of time to prepare. He cannot know before them."

Eva's mouth went dry. "A fondness?" Was she so transparent? Did everyone know? Did her brother know?

Nay, if he did, he'd have said something by now.

Cormac's lips lifted into a warm smile. "Aye, I see the way you look at each other. It's good that you've finally found a friend."

Eva felt a hot flush rise up her cheeks. "Please don't say anything to my brother," she whispered, hardly able to believe she was having such a conversation with a man who was all but a stranger to her.

Cormac's smile deepened into a mirthful grin. "Not a word," he promised. "But I'd also like your oath that you will keep news of our journey a secret."

"I swear I will not speak of it to anyone," Eva vowed.

"Sleep well, my lady," Cormac said, taking his leave.

She'd be lucky to sleep at all after that conversation. Eva flopped onto her bed, letting her gaze wander the wooden rafters of her single, small room.

Cormac knew there was *something* between her and Finn. Did he believe them to be courting? To be lovers? All he had said was friends, but Eva thought that might have been deliberately evasive on his part. Cormac was one of the cleverest men she'd met.

*Could* they be any of those things? For so long Eva believed her cousin, Baeth, would kill any man she dared to marry. Yet it had been years since she'd seen him, and even longer since he'd made any threats on her.

Perhaps he'd forgotten all about her. Perhaps he didn't even know where she was now. Perhaps she was finally free to marry.

Perhaps.

And what of this new trial of bravery? What if Finn died?

The very thought brought a sick feeling to her stomach, like a wrong movement would empty it of her dinner.

Eva sat up slowly, playing with her lips as she mused over the complexities of the situation. She knew, as Cormac had so casually stated, that she did have a fondness for Finn. After so many weeks together, Eva could hardly imagine what life would be like without him.

Before he came to Cenn Cora, Eva's life spiraled out of her control. Her cousin's actions forced her to forego her dreams of marriage in favor of a nunnery. Though she'd taken no vows, it had offered her respite from her troubles for a time. Then she'd been forced to offer herself as a hostage to secure the safety of her family.

Life in Brian's household, first in Caiseal and then in Cenn Cora, proved nearly unbearable. Everyone shunned her. No one wanted to be caught speaking with a Laigin noble. The servants hadn't even looked at her in Caiseal. They only did so in Cenn Cora out of the necessity of running the keep.

Broccan ignored her entirely. Cormac and Illadan had always been polite but maintained a distance. No matter how she tried to engage them in conversation, they always had some other place to go. Custom dictated that she sit on her own, as she was not a member of the family, but a trophy to be displayed, a symbol of victory and power. It hadn't been long before she stopped trying to change her lot.

But then Finn came to Cenn Cora. And her brother. And having them here changed everything. Suddenly, there were people who *wanted* her company, who cared about whether she ate her meals or walked too closely to the lake or enjoyed playing the harp.

It was as though the world had shifted when she met Finn, and somehow she now felt capable of standing on her own feet.

And Finn had joined the Fianna of his own desire, for his family. If something happened to him at the trial in Caiseal, it wouldn't be because of her dastardly cousin. It would be because Finn wanted to help his sister live without fear of abuse. Which, in Eva's estimation, was indeed a good cause for risking one's life, as much as she hated that he must do it.

Slipping out of her evening dress and under the cool linen sheets, Eva thought that if Finn made it through the trials, perhaps she might reconsider marriage.

Perhaps.

# CHAPTER TWENTY-FOUR

SWEAT POURED DOWN his brow. His legs ached. His ragged breath mirrored his ragged state. Finn dropped to the ground for the hundredth time since dawn, convinced he now had more mud plastered to his body than there was anywhere in the training course.

"Go, Finn!" Dallan roared from beside him. "Faster! Go faster!"

Rain pelted his back, dripping muddy rivulets down his face. He knew he wouldn't make it. Again.

He heard Diarmid and Conan join in shouting, cheering him on. Though he appreciated their support, it did little to change the fact that he'd finally come across a trial that was truly a challenge for him.

His head, and even his shoulders, he managed to barely squeeze beneath the branch. Just as he thought he was through, he heard Diarmid's dismayed cry. "Nay, Finn! Lower! You're going to—"

There was no need for him to finish his statement. Finn's backside caught the branch, knocking it to the ground. With a sigh he stood, wiping the mud from his face as he joined his friends.

He didn't even get a chance to ask for more advice. They spoke in unison, making it impossible to understand a single word until they slowed down. Dallan managed to get his thoughts in first.

"You must keep your hips down," he instructed. Again.

Finn threw his hands in the air. "I thought I was." He looked upward, letting the rain wash some of the muck from him as he tried not to give in to despair. "The trial is in three days," he lamented. "I don't know if I'm going to make it. How can *this* be the challenge I fail?"

All three heads shook vehemently in response. Arms waved, hands motioned. Diarmid even started picking up his legs to show Finn the proper technique which, for some unfathomable reason, he seemed utterly incapable of using.

"Lads," Conan shouted at last, silencing the chaos as though he were the king himself, "there's nothing for it. We're going to have to sit on him."

Finn looked up at him from hooded eyes. "You must be joking."

"I never jest about getting you sad lot through these incredibly simple trials," he replied with a smirk. "Diarmid, you're the smallest. You sit on him."

Diarmid's devilish grin did not bode well for Finn's pride. "Down you go, pony."

Dallan folded his arms, nodding reassuringly and doing his damndest not to crack a smile of his own.

Swallowing his rapidly diminishing pride, Finn set up to attempt the crawl again. The branch was halfway up his shin, below his knees. There was no earthly reason he shouldn't be able to flatten himself enough to make it underneath without catching it. And still he had yet to do so.

With far too much enthusiasm, Diarmid sat right over his hips, his long legs dragging beside Finn as he crawled through the squelching mud. Since he had Diarmid on his back, he crawled beside the branch instead of directly beneath it. And, though it frustrated him to no end, having Diarmid sit on him did, in fact, completely change his form. To get his belly anywhere near the ground, he had to splay out his legs from the hips, using the insides of his feet instead of his toes to gain traction.

When he stood, Dallan and Conan nodded approvingly.

"Now do *that* without Diarmid," Conan ordered sternly. "Same exact form."

He shook his head like a wet dog, flicking water droplets back into the rain.

He took a deep breath and, without letting himself think overmuch, he went for it. He dropped his belly to the ground. He splayed out his legs at the hips, so that the insides of his feet dragged beside him.

And, for the first time ever, he made it under the branch.

AFTER THEY'D FINISHED their morning training, Finn and Dallan cleaned up in the lake before heading into the village to commission Eva's harp. The entire way, Dallan offered suggestions for Finn to practice in order to gain speed and maintain the technique.

Finn listened gratefully, as it took his mind off the fact that they were headed into the village. He nodded, trying to focus on the meaning behind Dallan's words. In reality, only half of what his friend said penetrated his worries.

Finn was not a fearful man. Very few things unnerved him. One of those things being trips into the village. Any village, really. It never bothered Ethlinn, which is how she ended up running into Ernin more than the rest of the family.

Finn and his father stayed in and around their farm and the surrounding land. His mother and sister frequented town for supplies. Even in Cenn Cora, where he'd finally met men who did not judge him for his father's heritage, who accepted him as a true friend in spite of their many differences, even there he didn't dare venture away from the keep. Folk had a way of making him feel less than human when they took a long look at him and saw a foreigner.

As he'd told himself time and again, he could not blame them. It hurt him, yes, but they had no way of knowing his family had settled peacefully, had not taken part in the violence and terror most folk associated with the Ostmen. And it was a reputation well-deserved. That knowledge did little to assuage the sting of abject rejection, however.

"We should head to the carpenter?" Dallan asked as they strode into the center of the small village.

Finn sucked in a hesitant breath. "There's no harpmaker?"

Dallan snorted in amusement. "Have you seen the size of this place? *Village* is a generous term."

He wasn't wrong there, and Luimneach was too far a journey for them from Cenn Cora while the trials were underway. Not to mention Illadan's sudden, odd rule about not traveling too far during the trials. Reluctantly, Finn nodded agreement. "The carpenter it is. If he's incapable, the bowyer may work as well."

"You do the talking," Dallan muttered as they approached the carpenter's hut. "I've no idea where to even begin."

The carpenter, whom Finn knew as Tómma from Eva's stories of rebuilding the keep's kitchen, watched them approach with a wary eye. Finn smiled in greeting, moving to pull his harp from his pack.

"Well met, Master Tómma," Finn greeted him as warmly as he could, given the glare the man leveled at him. "We'd like to commission a harp, if that's something you can do."

Tómma spit on the ground in front of him, still giving Finn and Dallan a dark, sidelong glance. "No."

A tightness threatened to take hold in Finn's chest, yet he knew he was overreacting. Likely the man wasn't denying him personally, though it certainly felt that way.

"Oh," Finn mumbled, carefully composing his next attempt. He knew Dallan wouldn't leave the village until they'd found *someone* to make the harp. "That's no trouble. They're not terribly difficult for a master carpenter like yourself."

Silence. And a deeper furrow in the obstinate man's brow.

Finn looked askance at Dallan, who nodded encouragingly. Dallan backed down from no challenge, as far as Finn could tell.

Taking a deep breath, Finn tried once again. "I'm sorry if I've offended you in some way. Lady Eva assured us you were the best at what you do. If you're uncomfortable taking on an odd project, I'd be happy to sit and discuss the finer points of harp construction with you. We'll pay you well for your troubles."

"I said no," Tómma repeated firmly, irritation clear in his tone. "And my skills are not the trouble. I won't be making a harp for any Ostman, who's no business owning or playing an instrument so sacred to the people you've slaughtered."

Stunned into silence, Finn had no chance of stopping Dallan from lunging toward the startled carpenter.

Dallan grabbed two fistfuls of the man's shirt, picking him up bodily and pressing him against the outside of his cottage. "What did you just say to my friend?"

Undaunted, Tómma continued. "If you're friends with him, I'd say much the same to you."

"You cocksure bastard," Dallan spat, angrier than Finn had ever seen him. "I came here today hoping to pay handsomely for a craftsman's best work, not threaten one into behaving like a man instead of a pile of shite."

"Hit me, then, if it pleases you. But I won't be making anything for a foreign brute and his guard."

"Dallan," Finn interrupted, worried it might get out of hand, "we can find someone else. He's not worth it." He had expected this sort of treatment. He had never thought Dallan would take up the fight on his behalf.

Still holding the carpenter by his léine, Dallan turned his head halfway round toward Finn. "He cannot insult you thus without recompense."

"He's not the first to do so, and surely won't be the last," Finn argued resignedly.

Turning back to Tómma, Dallan's voice grew dangerously low. "I'm not going to hit you old man," he growled. "I'm going to make sure no one ever buys from a man stupid enough to deny the Prince of Laigin a harp on account of the company he keeps."

Tómma's eyes went wide. "The Prince of..." he trailed off,

looking first at Dallan, then at Finn, then back to Dallan, swallowing hard and looking rather pale. "My apologies, my lord," he stuttered. "If you'll release me, I'd very much like to speak with your friend here of the makings of a quality harp. I'll have no less for two such—cultured men."

"There's more to it than that now, carpenter," Dallan continued, letting go of the man's crumpled léine. "I'll still pay you handsomely for your fine work, but you'll be taking on a second job in addition."

"Of course," Tómma replied before Dallan had finished speaking. "Anything to help you."

"You'll be making sure everyone in this village knows that Finn here is indeed an Ostman, and one of the most loyal, brave, and fierce men I've ever met. He will soon be one of the king's Fianna, defending your sorry arse should there be any true threats to your safety. I shouldn't have to remind anyone of this, as he has done nothing to deserve your insolence. See that it is so."

"Happily, my lord."

After sitting down with the carpenter and gaining his cooperation, Finn quickly realized that the man could indeed do the job they required. He had made several some years past and knew enough of their form and function and the types of wood required to do a fine job.

The return walk to the village proved awkward, for Finn at least. What could he say to such a service as Dallan had done him? He was a true friend, Finn thought, and for the first time in his life Finn felt truly accepted by the people around him.

Dallan, Cormac, Diarmid, and Eva all treated him as one of them.

The thought of Eva brought a sharp twinge of guilt to Finn's chest. He needed to tell Dallan the truth. He needed to admit his feelings to his friend. Had Dallan not acclaimed him as loyal?

Hardly, at present. But he could start now.

Decision made, he cleared his throat. "I've been talking with Eva lately of her past betrothals," he began tentatively. "Have you ever considered arranging another match for her, should she want one?"

"Never," Dallan answered too quickly. "And see her heart broken yet again? Nay, she made me vow to leave her be. That's why she went to the nunnery. Not for the Lord, but for solace and distance."

"But what if she changed her mind?"

"She won't," Dallan assured him. "And, honestly, I'd have to beat any bastard who tried. The only way she'd agree is if he'd already charmed her by some miracle, and I can't abide that thought."

Finn's stomach soured. Dallan's assessment struck true. His mind fumbled the remainder of the short walk for any way to explain his relationship with Eva, but it always came up wanting.

By the time they'd reached the tents, Finn had convinced himself it wasn't worthwhile to rile Dallan over nothing. As he'd said, Eva had no interest in marriage, which meant she had no interest in courting either.

Which meant that upsetting Dallan over something that would never amount to aught would only create unnecessary tension. Eva had told him as much herself. Hadn't she said she still wasn't ready to consider marriage?

He fooled only himself in thinking she would change her mind for an Ostman peasant. So, he said nothing.

Determined, he vowed not to let anything further happen with Eva.

# CHAPTER TWENTY-FIVE

EVA WAS FAIRLY certain no one would die today. At least she could count on that. She also thought her pig-headed brother had a fair chance of failing the trial. She could only hope, anyway.

She'd had Finn explain it to her several times over, both the trial itself and the training they did to prepare for it. And still she could not comprehend how any person could do such a thing as leap over a tree.

As in the trial of defense, wherein the men defended themselves from spears in holes deep as their waists, this trial, too, necessitated the accommodation of each individual man. In order for each to undergo the same level of challenge, each man had found a branch of the proper length to be stuck into the ground and of a height with him. On the other side of each branch, a branch lower than their knees and higher than their ankles waited, suspended between a pair of much smaller branches. In order to succeed the trial, a man must jump over the tall branch and crawl beneath the lower one without touching them.

She, without the need to attempt it, knew she couldn't do either. Based on the chatter surrounding her, she was not the only soul watching who thought as much. Finn had tried once, after she'd continued to question him, to get Eva to try jumping at least. She told him in no uncertain terms she preferred the harp to any sort of physical challenge.

He always offered. Whenever Eva spoke of something beyond her ken, to the best of his ability Finn presented her with an opportunity to learn it, to practice it, to better understand it. Since learning of her inability to swim, he had also suggested swimming lessons. She'd managed to convince him to put those off for now.

In truth, she had no desire whatsoever to learn to swim. She was perfectly content to stand upon the shore and gaze at the beauty of the water without ever breaking its surface. If, for some reason, she *must* touch it, dangling her feet would more than suffice. Even that set her nerves on edge. As much as Finn loved to remind her to be careful, it was hardly necessary. Eva was well aware of the danger if she fell.

The men took their positions behind the tall branches, each with his own, drawing her attention from her own musings. A clap of thunder sounded in the distance, and the sky clouded over ominously, but no storm yet came. Cormac nodded to the first of the twenty-two men, who, to Eva's shock, jumped straight up and over the branch.

A collective gasp sounded from the crowd, followed by cheers as he crawled on his belly under the branch. Out of breath, he stood victorious. The crowd roared, hungry for more.

The next men went, attempting the same. Two failed and two succeeded before Finn's turn.

Eva held her breath, her hands squeezing each other so hard her nails dug into her skin.

Finn didn't even hesitate. The confidence in his hard stare made her heart swell with pride. He leaped over the branch. And he made it look effortless. He paused only a heartbeat before dropping onto the ground and crawling under the branch with practiced ease.

Everyone cheered again, their raucous enjoyment of the sport gaining momentum with each man's turn. Finn grinned, his single dimple visible even from a distance. His fellow competitors, those who had already completed their trials, came up to congratulate him. But Finn paid them little heed. His eyes searched the crowd until they found Eva, piercing her with a questioning gaze.

She stood with the rest of the onlookers, clapping and smiling like a fool. Even with the entire village cheering him on, he desired her approval. Eva didn't have time to contemplate that confusing thought. For all of the applause for Finn ended in a matter of moments, and her brother stepped up for his turn.

Once more, her breath hitched as his entire body worked in unison to propel him over the branch. The bastard managed the jump. And the crawl. Everyone around her shouted in encouragement, but Eva only clapped absently, frowning. She was proud of her brother, but if he didn't fail a trial soon, he'd force her to make a decision she'd been putting off for some time now. A decision that grew more complicated with each passing day.

An idea had formed in her mind in the weeks since she'd met Finn's sister, Ethlinn. She'd nursed it along, letting it take root during the time she and Finn had stopped meeting.

Ethlinn had tried so hard, been so clever in her attempts to get Finn away from the trials. But, like Eva's own stubborn brother, he hadn't budged. Eva had even confronted Dallan, something Ethlinn had directly avoided, and that had done naught to sway him. She realized that to succeed she needed far more drastic action. She needed to reinforce her own sacrifice, to ensure her position as hostage would not be traded away to her brother against her will.

At one point she had considered begging permission to travel back to Caiseal and speak with Brian on the matter, hoping he'd heed Sitric's original submission over Dallan's counter-offer. After Finn had started meeting with her again, bringing joy and passion into her life for the first time in years, Eva had selfishly pushed thoughts of Brian and Dallan and hostageship to the back of her mind.

She'd told herself it was because Dallan would most likely fail one of the upcoming trials, saving her the trouble of ousting him. Until now, she hadn't been able to admit the truth.

Finn made her want to marry again, made her believe the life she'd always imagined still lay within reach. He gave her hope.

And if she remained Brian's hostage, marriage would be out of the question. Or so she had told herself, before she'd been willing to reconsider her stance on it.

Watching Finn and Dallan rejoice with their friends, cheering and shouting and grinning like fools, Eva wondered if perhaps she could manage both. What if, instead of asking Brian only to keep her on as a hostage, she also asked for permission to marry one of his Fianna?

For with each passing trial, Eva felt more and more that Finn would be among the last men standing. And, Lord help her, she hoped he bested them all.

AFTER THE MEN had all attempted the trial, eight of the two-and-twenty had failed, leaving fourteen to pass on to the next trial in a fortnight's time. That evening, after the men had washed all the dirt and sweat from themselves, they celebrated another victory feast in the hall.

Eva wore a pale blue gown with gold embroidery and white trim. Finn had requested several days earlier that she cease wearing the cream one, excepting a true emergency. She'd teased him over that, but in truth his request had stung. She knew he still felt guilty over keeping their trysts from her brother, for which she could hardly fault him. Indeed, his chivalrous behavior was one of the things she admired most about him.

By the time the feasting had begun, the storm erupted in earnest. Flashes of lightning tore through a darkening sky and thunder cracked like a falling oak, yet still the rain held out. Such storms happened every now and then, blowing through with the bluster falling short of the promised potential.

All through the meal, the hungry looks Finn gave her had her wishing he'd not banned their private meetings. He'd said naught about dancing, however, and Eva had every intention of coercing him back onto the dance floor. She wasn't about to go the entire night without being in his arms, even if it was only for a short dance.

As the servants cleared the empty platters and pushed the tables to the perimeter of the room to make space for dancing, Dallan and Cormac approached Eva. Dallan carried a wheat sack as though it were made of gold.

"Cormac's allowed me to speak with you briefly this eve," he explained, handing her the sack. "I commissioned this for you. I hope it's to your liking."

Eva carefully removed the rough covering from the mysterious object. She drew in a sharp breath, gazing down at the ornately carved harp she now held. Tapping a string, as Finn had taught her, she fought to keep tears from her eyes.

"You needn't have gone to such trouble," she whispered, her voice breaking.

Dallan pulled her into a gentle hug. "Consider it a very late nameday gift."

"It's beautiful, Dallan. Thank you."

"Finn came with me to ensure it was done properly. It should be a good size for you, or so he tells me. If it's not, we'll get it adjusted. But now you can practice whenever you'd like."

Eva couldn't put to words the depth of emotion swirling within her. It felt as though Dallan had handed her the key to her own freedom. For, even if she remained a hostage and Finn a distant memory, at least she could still play. In that way, she'd always be thinking of him and his beautiful music.

"I'll start tonight," she promised. "I'm sure Finn will be relieved not to share his own harp anymore. Perhaps we can play a duet now."

Dallan chuckled. "I thought I'd never get him to agree to teaching you," he remarked, as though it were a change in the weather. "I begged him for days before he agreed, but I knew you'd always wanted to learn. And there's no better teacher than Finn. Don't you think? We're lucky to have met him."

A hole opened in Eva's chest, threatening to cave in her entire being. Some small voice in her head whispered that her brother jested with her. He always jested. But that voice drowned in the waves of shock and embarrassment that now threatened to overwhelm her.

Her mouth went dry. She looked at Finn, smiling at her from across the room.

He'd lied to her.

God's bones, her chest ached. Her stomach heaved as though she might lose her dinner there and then. Of course, he'd lied. Had she expected him to say as much to her face? Of course, he'd pitied her.

Mortification and anger warred within her as Dallan said his goodbyes and returned to the rest of the men.

Leaving the harp in the alcove they frequented, Eva skirted the edge of the crowded room and raced out the door. Another clap of thunder sounded as she rushed headlong toward the lake, the first drops of rain not far behind it.

# CHAPTER TWENTY-SIX

FINN WATCHED EVA slip into the crowd as Dallan returned to his side. Something about her expression gave him pause. She turned away so quickly it was difficult to see her clearly, yet his gut told him she was upset. But hadn't Dallan just given her the harp? How could that be?

"What's wrong with Eva?" Finn asked as soon as Dallan came near enough to hear him over the murmur of the crowd. "Didn't she like it?"

Dallan cast him a sideways glance, eyebrow raised. "She loved it," he answered. "Why?"

Finn looked again across the room but had lost sight of Eva. "She just seemed upset as you were leaving is all."

Dallan grinned. "Well, who wouldn't be?" he jested. "She's fine, Finn. She was so happy she looked about to cry; mayhap that's what you saw."

Finn wanted that to be true. But something still didn't feel right. "What was the last thing you said to her?" It had been right before Dallan left that her face had fallen.

"Good eve."

Finn shot him a dark look.

"Fine, fine," Dallan acquiesced, raising his hands. "I told her she was lucky to have you as a teacher."

There had to be more. "And before that?"

"You need an ale, you know that?"

"Dallan, please humor me."

"I think I made some joke about how hard it was to get you to teach her initially. She was getting so emotional over the harp, I had to say something light-hearted," Dallan explained. "It's my job as the brother, you know. Making sure she always has a good laugh."

A brick's weight of fear hit Finn full force. No wonder she'd been upset. He'd assured her a hundred times over the past months that he truly enjoyed teaching her. That he *wanted* to teach her.

Finn ran a hand down his face in frustration. She'd never believe him now.

He couldn't explain all that to Dallan, however, and there was no need to worry him unnecessarily. Perhaps he could find her and explain. He had to try.

"I'm going to go see how she likes it," Finn said after several moments. Excusing himself just as Diarmid and Conan joined them, he hurried over to the alcove where he met with Eva for their lessons.

She wasn't there.

But her harp was.

It lay atop the chair she always used, abandoned.

Finn took a deep breath. He would not panic. There was nothing to panic over. He simply needed to find her, explain what had happened, and everything would be fine. He surveyed the room again, still unable to find any trace of Eva amongst the revelers. He picked up the harp and started walking to see more of the hall. A passing kitchen maid, a girl of no more than ten-and-three summers with shiny, chestnut braids hanging down her back, gave him an idea. Finn intercepted her.

"Did you happen to see where Lady Eva went?" he asked.

The girl shook her head, her chestnut-colored braids smacking her back. "I only just came from the kitchens. She was leaving as I came in."

She'd left.

And there was only one place she would go when she was so

upset.

"Thank you," Finn muttered hastily, weaving his way through the crowd to the door. By the time he reached the courtyard, rain fell in heavy sheets, turning the buildings into waterfalls and the courtyard into a mess of mud and stone. Between the fading daylight and the torrential rain, Finn could hardly see an arm's length in front of him.

If the courtyard was already a muddy pit, the trail down to the lake would be a veritable river.

Taking off at a sprint, Finn flew toward the forest, praying he wasn't too late.

THE STING OF Finn's betrayal only deepened as Eva ran through the rain. The pain in her chest swirled like smoke, a cavernous ache following its writhing grasp. He had lied to her. And worse, he did pity her.

Eva paused when she finally broke free of the keep's outbuildings. She stood and let the rain pelt her, the cool water helping to calm her raging emotions. Once she'd had some time alone to think, she would know what to do. Right now, she needed to be down at the lake.

Reaching the canopy of trees, Eva felt her nerves begin to calm. Even in the pouring rain, even with thunder cracking angrily overhead, she could breathe again.

Her thoughts wandered far afield, grappling with the worry that all the trust she'd placed in Finn, all the moments they'd shared had been based upon a lie.

As she walked, however, Eva's surroundings forced her to focus on her journey down the trail. The top of the trail was the same as always, if muddier. The further she went, the less stable it grew. Nearing the stone where she waited for Finn, she realized she needed to turn back. She could already hear the churning water just beyond the nearby tree line, the sound of angry waves pounding the rocky shore reaching her even in her despair.

Eva turned to head back up the trail, only to find it had become a tiny but powerful stream of mud and raging runoff.

Determined not to panic, though she had to admit it wasn't looking good, Eva reached for the nearest tree to support her as she climbed upward against the current.

Her left foot slipped. Her right foot couldn't hold her. She felt the rough bark of the tree brush her fingers just before the muddy water carried her away.

# CHAPTER TWENTY-SEVEN

COLD. FRIGID COLD. Heart racing, nerves striking her body like the lightning overhead.

She couldn't swim. And she was in the lake.

Thunder cracked. Her arms reached, her neck stiffened. She couldn't breathe, she couldn't shout. The water's surface bobbed just out of reach no matter the effort she made.

One breath, finally. Then a mouthful of muddy water. Eva choked, trying to spit it out. Instead, she took in more through her nose.

Her legs kicked. Her arms grabbed, as if she could touch the shore, though she couldn't even see it. For all she knew she'd washed to the next village over already. Her body moved as it willed, no longer controlled by her mind.

Against the chaos of the raging waters, a moment of tranquility settled upon Eva. In the depths of her mind, she knew she would die. Her efforts at escape paled pitifully in the face of the roiling waves. She could not free herself.

Yet the panic faded, even in the face of this knowledge. The more imminent her death became, the easier it grew to accept her fate. Instead of struggling, Eva settled into a trance under the water.

Her dress billowed about her, swirling in the undertow. Bubbles trailed in its wake. The flashes of lightning overhead illuminated the translucent waves and bubbles, creating a breathtaking landscape of light and dark that mesmerized Eva.

From the darkness two shadows emerged, moving rapidly toward her. She heard nothing but the cacophonous tumult of stormy water.

An iron grip encircled first one arm, then the other, lifting her from her peaceful perch beneath the waves. She tried to protest, only to discover she could do naught but cough and choke, unable to draw a full breath. Chaos descended once more, the thunder above a stark reminder that escaping the waves did not guarantee safety.

The world spun about her in a whirlwind of water, reaching for her from the lake below and the sky above. The moment her feet hit land she threw herself to the ground, coughing up enough water to make a puddle on the muddy shore.

Several good whacks reverberated from her back through her body. Taking one gasping, ragged breath, Eva turned to see Finn behind her. His hands held her tightly, one about her waist, the other on her back. Even in her state of confusion, Eva noted how pale he'd gone, his face whiter than new milk. His hair lay plastered to his face by the torrential rain falling about them. Eyes the same grey-blue as the storm-tossed lake simmered at her with intensity.

Eva thought he might shout at her, but a sadness overtook the flash of anger on his face. He leaned forward, his hands pulling her head to his. "I thought I'd lost you," he whispered into her hair, barely audible over the storm. "I can't lose you."

Bit by bit, Eva's senses returned to her. She sank into Finn's warm body, his heart beating so hard she could feel its rhythm against her own chest.

He had saved her.

She had nearly drowned, and Finn had rescued her.

Eva's hopes soared. He had passed some of the most challenging physical trials, leaping over trees as big as a man, defending himself from an onslaught of spears with naught but a shield and his own considerable skill. He had proven his intellect through his dedication to music and poetry. And, when she'd needed him most, he had been there. Though she hardly dared believe it possible, it seemed that Finn could handle anything.

And at this very moment, sitting in his arms on the shore, soaked to the bone and coughing up water, Eva decided that perhaps he could handle her family as well. It had been an awfully long time since her cousin had caused any mischief. As long as they kept their betrothal a secret, Eva felt they would be perfectly safe.

A flush of heat rose within her as she held his words close. *I can't lose you.*

In that instant, Eva knew she couldn't lose him either. If there were a way to make a marriage between them work, she would find it. She gazed up at him, raindrops running down her face. "No," she agreed, "you can't." She raised her hand to his face, tracing the strong line of his jaw until his eyes met hers. "I'm beginning to think you can survive anything, Finn Ulfsson."

Finn's breathing grew shallow. He clearly understood her implication. "Even marrying you?" he asked, his voice rough with emotion.

"Aye," she grinned, suddenly not caring a whit about the tempestuous storm assaulting them, "even marrying me."

Finn's lips fell on hers, desperate and hungry. She needed to be close to him, to taste him, to touch him. In his arms, she felt safe. She felt loved. She felt that, in spite of the insecurities in this life, she had a haven to call home. His hands untied the stays in her gown, her heart pounding again. This time, it wasn't in fear.

The chill rain kissed every inch of her that Finn missed, her skin turning to gooseflesh as his lips worshipped first her neck, then her shoulder.

Eva shivered as a gust of wind sent a volley of icy raindrops toward them.

Finn covered her with his own body, moving to lay atop her and shield her from the raging storm. A droplet of water fell from his hair, landing squarely on her nose. She giggled as he wiped the drop away. He grinned at her in return, his eyes clouded with hunger. He smelled like grass after it rains, earthy and crisp and surreal.

"You're warm," she whispered in his ear, so he could hear her over the chaotic weather. Cupping his face in her hands, she stared so deeply into his blue eyes she felt she could fall into them. "Would you really marry me, Finn?"

He pulled her hand to his mouth, soft lips kissing first the back of her hand, then her palm. Another wave of heat shot through her, her breath catching as his eyes devoured her and his lips scandalized her. "Would you really let me?" he countered.

"Baeth hasn't bothered us in years," she reasoned. "I think I may finally be free to marry without trouble from him."

"And if he does?"

Eva shivered again at that thought. She would never be ready to lose another loved one to her cousin's thirst for violence, but she doubted he would resurface after so long in silence. Finn pitted against Baeth still felt unimaginable. Luckily, it didn't matter any longer.

"He won't," she insisted, "but if he does, I believe only one of the Fianna could defeat him."

Finn's laugh brought out his single, adorable dimple. "I'm not a *fénnid* yet," he cautioned.

"You will be." Eva knew it deep in her bones, felt the truth of it. "I've not seen a warrior so accomplished in all my life. You'll pass the trials, Finn, of that I have no doubt."

"Would you want me if I didn't?"

Eva saw the vulnerability in his face, the question in his eyes. She saw the young boy inside the man, the one who had been an outsider his whole life in spite of his many talents.

The one who had seen her at her worst and still believed in her.

"I will always want you, Finn," she told him in the Ostman language, "whether you're a bard or a farmer or a *fénnid,* we will belong with each other."

Another crack of thunder reminded Eva of their tenuous

position in the shelter of a swaying pine.

"We should head back," Finn began.

Eva's kiss interrupted him. Right now, all she wanted was more time alone with Finn. Storm be damned. "I need you," she whispered between kisses, her hands sneaking under his soaking léine.

His breath grew ragged as his hands worked to free her from her sodden gown.

Eva pulled him down atop her, warmed by his hard body even in the relentless winds. She sighed, arching her back as his hands explored her soaking skin, his mouth following behind, lighting her on fire.

Nothing mattered but getting closer to Finn. An aching as she had never known bloomed deep within her. She needed to feel his touch again.

But she also wanted more.

Eva gasped as Finn took one of her nipples into his mouth, his hand moving purposefully down toward her thighs. This time when he pulled her skirts up and reached beneath them, Eva didn't protest. Instead, she reached for the waistline of his trews.

"Eva," Finn's ragged whisper sent a shiver of excitement through her.

His voice alone melted her. She dipped a finger beneath the taut fabric until she grazed something hard and smooth.

"Eva," he repeated, his voice filled with dangerous promise, "if we do that, we'll be married indeed, even if not by law."

"We'll be lovers?" she asked, undeterred.

"Aye," he confirmed. "Do you know what that means? I know that sometimes daughters are not—"

"I don't," she interrupted gently, "but I'd like you to show me." She didn't know precisely what that meant, but Eva knew she liked everything Finn had taught her about love thus far.

The rain had died down around them, falling in staccato bursts from the branches of the towering pine.

Lightning crackled in the distance, thunder following as it

always does. The storm around them had moved on, but the storm within Eva was only beginning.

As Finn's fingers toyed with her most intimate places, Eva ran her hand down his hard length, eliciting a groan that emboldened her further. With several tugs she managed to get his trews off.

The more attention he gave her, however, the more difficulty she had focusing. He caught her moan with a kiss as he lowered himself toward her, positioning his manhood where his fingers had been mere moments earlier.

Slowly, he entered her.

Eva needed more. "Finn," she begged, lifting her hips to bring him deeper inside her.

Every muscle in his body tightened against her. He moved in deeper in one swift thrust, surprising her with the pain of it.

Even as she thought to tell him, the discomfort ebbed.

He brought his hand between them, his finger circling her most sensitive area while he held perfectly still inside her. She felt him throbbing, heard his strained breathing—this man who was one of the fittest in the kingdom—as he used all his will to wait for her comfort. Desire swelled in her again, an ache that began in her stomach and pooled where his finger worked. She lifted her hips again, and this time Finn caught them in his hands.

He moved inside her faster, faster, each thrust as electric as a strike of lightning. Eva cried out as the storm within her broke, reaching for Finn. He thrust deep inside her one final time before collapsing into her outstretched arms.

He lifted his head enough to touch his forehead to her own, his hand playing with her hair.

She smiled at him, kissing his nose. She felt as though she could take on the whole world, as though no problem would be too much as long as she had Finn.

Finn sat up, pulling her into his lap and wrapping his arms about her. With a sigh, he lowered his chin on her head.

"What's wrong?" she asked, suddenly rather self-conscious. She'd never done that before, and though she'd thoroughly enjoyed it, perhaps he hadn't. "Did I do it wrong?"

He chuckled and she felt his head shaking above hers. "That was incredible," he told her. "You did it exactly right."

"Then what's wrong?"

"I just realized that your brother is probably going to kill me."

Eva choked back a laugh. "Don't tell him yet," she replied. "I will ask Brian if he would consider allowing us to marry first. And I can tell my brother we are to be wed so he has no opportunity for murder."

"We should tell him together," Finn's tone told her of the import of the statement. "If it were my sister, I'd want to hear it from him, too."

Eva nodded. She understood that. Finn and Dallan had grown close over the past months, and Finn's loyalty to her brother was something that had endeared him to her from the beginning.

But asking permission from Brian and Dallan was a problem for tomorrow.

Tonight belonged to Finn, and Eva planned to spend all of it with him.

# CHAPTER TWENTY-EIGHT

FINN SWORE AGAIN as yet another thorn pierced tender flesh on the bottom of his foot. He heard Dallan do the same just behind him as they raced through the forest surrounding Cenn Cora. Summer had reached its height, surpassed it, even, and the whole world glowed a bright, sun-drenched green. The midday sun shone hot, high overhead in a clear blue sky. A series of late season storms had ushered in a layer of new growth, promising a challenging run through the wooded hillside.

The thought of a rainstorm, and the delicious memories that accompanied it, distracted Finn. He stepped on a second thorn, gritting his teeth and keeping his pace. Stepping on a thorn was only the first part of the upcoming trial. After stepping upon the thorn, he had to remove it without slowing down. A simple task, but not an easy one as it turned out.

Finn broke through the tree line at the top of the hill moments before Dallan.

"Did you do it?" Conan asked, walking over to Dallan.

Of the four of them, Dallan struggled the greatest with this particular trial.

Diarmid strode confidently across the field, joining them near the forest's shadowy edge. He stretched out his arms in a dramatic gesture. "Well?" he pressed.

Dallan grimaced, shaking his head of dark curls. "This trial will be the death of me," he uttered angrily.

"We warned you," Finn teased, letting his hand fall heavily

on Dallan's shoulder.

"It's true. We did," Diarmid added with a wicked grin.

Finn had stopped trying to keep count of how many ladies had already succumbed to Diarmid's considerable charm. His playful manner and quick smile had kept him quite busy in the evenings.

Dallan ran a hand down his face, pulling his features into a picture of frustration. "Two days," he groaned. "I have two days to get the damned thorn out without tripping."

"Get a drink, take a walk, and meet us back here for more," Conan ordered. "We won't let you fail now."

"If sitting on you would help, you know I'd do it," Diarmid offered.

Dallan looked daggers at him but made no comment.

Finn gave him a push toward the drinking bucket, where a supply of water was kept close at hand for the men during training. Conan and Diarmid wandered nearer the keep, promising to return to further torment Dallan.

"I'll fetch us some food," Finn offered. He knew Dallan's feet would be twice as sore as his own after so many passes through the bramble. Dallan only had two days to train, though the trial itself wasn't for four more days. The men's feet needed to heal enough that new wounds would be distinguishable from the old, a testament to the thorn they must step on to pass the trial.

Nearing the kitchens, the sound of harp music floated from the row of buildings just beyond the feasting hall. Finn stilled, listening.

It was Eva.

He knew the sound of her music as he knew the taste of her lips and the feel of her in his arms. Stepping on thorns was nothing compared with the agony of leaving Eva last night, let alone pretending nothing had happened all morning as he trained alongside Dallan. They had met nearly every eve following their lessons, and she assured him she had a plan. He only hoped she spoke with Brian soon; he hated keeping their secret from his best friend.

Even as he had trained, racing headlong until he could hardly breathe, Finn struggled to keep thoughts of Eva from his mind. All he wanted to do was go to her, but he knew Dallan needed his help. Glancing back toward the training field, Finn spotted Dallan sprawled on the ground staring at the cloudless sky. He'd be fine for a moment.

Finn walked past the kitchens, following the unfamiliar melody to Eva's door. He decided to only open it a crack, so he didn't disturb her while she played. As soon as he moved the door, however, the music halted abruptly.

"Finn!" Eva leaped from her chair, harp cast onto her bed, and nearly threw herself into Finn's arms. She seemed to remember at the same time as Finn that they were meant to be secretive about their tryst. Backing away awkwardly, she smiled at him instead.

"I've never heard that song," Finn explained. "I had to come to listen to it."

"It's my own composition." She lifted her chin, clearly pleased with her work.

And rightly so. It was a beautiful melody, filled with movement and depth.

"Will there be words?"

A rosy blush spotted her pale cheeks. She nodded, rolling her lips together.

"I won't pry," Finn assured her. Perhaps the lyrics yet needed work. "But you should know it's already a wonderful piece."

"How is your training going? Will you pass the trial?" she asked.

Finn didn't miss her rush to change the subject. He wouldn't pry now, but her hedging only intensified his curiosity. "I will," he replied, certain of the truth of his statement. "The real question is: will Dallan?"

Her mouth dropped open, her eyes bright. She clapped her hands together beneath her chin. "Really!"

Finn snorted in amusement. "You know, one would think his sister might wish him well in his endeavors."

"I wish him well alright," Eva replied, "and if he's to stay that way he needs to get out of here. If losing one of those trials is what it takes, then that makes my job easier."

Finn leaned against the door frame. He shouldn't linger much longer, but he couldn't bring himself to leave. He *wanted* to throw her on the bed behind her and spend all afternoon tangled up with her in it.

"Have you thought about what you'll do if he does pass all the trials?"

Eva shook her head, her mouth pursed like she'd eaten a sour berry. "No. I should have a plan in place, but every time I think of something I also see why it won't work. My best idea so far is to simply beg Brian not to honor the agreement with Dallan and uphold the one made with Sitric instead." She shrugged, the light in her eyes fading. "Perhaps it is a fool's hope to believe I can protect him."

"Perhaps," Finn began carefully. "Even if he weren't joining the Fianna, would he not be a warrior in your uncle's forces? Risking his life just the same?"

Eva shot him a dark look. "At least then he'd be doing it for the family," she argued. "Now if he dies, it will be because of me."

Finn shook his head. He knew she wanted to protect her brother. He understood that. He had siblings and he would die for any one of them. But he also didn't want this self-imposed yoke to weigh her down for the rest of her days. For, in all likelihood, Dallan would manage to pass all the trials. He was easily among the best men competing.

"Nay," he pressed, not wanting to argue but knowing its necessity. "It will be because of him. Dallan made the decision. He made it because he loves you, but it was his to make."

Just as Finn had come here to help his own sister live a better life, free from fear. He knew it was a risk, but it was a risk worth taking.

"Why did you come here?" Eva asked, her eyes searching his own. "I know Ethlinn was attacked, and I suspect you were rejected by the bardic masters as an apprentice for some unholy reason, but what actually made you come here with my brother? What pushed you to risk so much?"

Finn smiled softly. "I've often wondered the same myself," he replied. "At first, it was anger. I felt such rage that Ethlinn had been beaten and my family could do nothing to protect her because of our standing, our lack of money or power. I was angry that I had been cast aside after eighteen years of study because my father was an Ostman…"

Eva gasped at that, fully interrupting him and not looking the least contrite. "*That* is why they rejected you?" she shouted, her fists clenching. "Because of your parents?"

"'No king will want a bard who's heart lay with the enemy,'" he repeated the master's frank words. "He was convinced I'd never be accepted as an advisor, which meant apprenticing me would be a waste of effort and resources. The worst part is that I couldn't tell my family that. I couldn't go home and say that to my father."

Eva's lips parted as understanding dawned. "That was when they gave you the harp," she thought aloud. "Just before they believed you'd be leaving to apprentice."

Finn nodded, "And just before we realized we needed those funds for Ethlinn."

No one—not Ethlinn, not even Dallan—knew the entirety of what had happened. Dallan knew he'd been rejected, of course, or he wouldn't have approached him. But he hadn't been privy to Finn's quiet conversation with the master. Only Eva knew what had really happened that night. Finn trusted her, with his heart and with his secrets.

"I can't help those fools see what they've lost in passing you over," Eva told him, righteous fury overtaking her angelic face, "but I can try to help Ethlinn. No matter what happens over the next weeks, I will do my best to ensure Ethlinn is safe."

"You can?" Finn didn't ask why she hadn't mentioned this earlier. It didn't matter. "How?"

"You may not have any connections or wealth, but Dallan and I both do. I don't know why I didn't think of this sooner." She started pacing the room, clearly running the possibilities through her mind. "Let me think on it more. It's not for certain, as I am somewhat limited in my reach currently. We can discuss it tonight after dinner."

Her simple green gown swished about her as she walked, accentuating the many curves with which Finn was now intimately familiar. She worried her bottom lip temptingly as she went. Finn couldn't take much more torment. He could sneak a kiss before he left. He took a step toward her.

"Where's the food?" Finn and Eva both jumped when Dallan appeared in the courtyard behind Finn. He grinned when he saw Eva's harp. "Was she playing?" he asked Finn excitedly.

Finn laughed nervously. Gods, he'd been about to kiss Eva. He let his head fall back a moment, grateful Dallan hadn't walked in on Finn kissing his little sister, guilty that he kept such a big secret from his friend. Hopefully, Eva spoke with Brian soon.

He couldn't take much more of this.

✿━━━━━━━━━━✿

# CHAPTER TWENTY-NINE

FINN SAT ON the hilltop, along the edge of the field where the men had been training for months, resting after a grueling afternoon of more sprinting through the forest. The warm breeze carried birdsong up the hill. The sound of footsteps told him he was no longer alone.

Turning, he watched Dallan stalk toward him, a dark look on his face.

Finn's stomach flipped. Had Dallan discovered his relationship with Eva? What would he say when Dallan inevitably confronted him? Each breath came more rapidly than the last as Dallan neared.

"You're no fool," he declared, finally reaching Finn but not sitting to join him.

Finn swallowed, trying to remain calm until he knew for certain what had Dallan so riled. "Thank you?" he replied, unsure what to make of Dallan's odd statement.

"I'm aware that you followed me here, knowing you didn't have the whole of my story and motives. But, as a true friend, you never pressed me for them. I know, in part, it was because coming here served your purposes as well. Today I will tell you everything, I swear it. But first, I must ask one more favor of you."

Finn stood. He'd never heard Dallan speak in such a manner, serious and straightforward, no hint of guile or amusement. "I will do anything you ask."

Dallan placed a hand on Finn's shoulder. "I knew I could count on you. Truly, you are a great friend." He nodded in the direction of the fortress. "Follow me."

A sinking feeling in the pit of his stomach nearly had Finn confessing about Eva. He realized this was not the right moment, that Dallan was not in the best place to learn such news. "Will you tell me where we're going?" he asked instead.

"My cousin, Baeth, is in Cenn Cora. He's as bloodthirsty as they come, and he's demanded an audience with me. He refuses to allow any of Brian's men inside, because he obviously is trying to start a rebellion, so Cormac has allowed you to stand in their place. Plus, I need a witness in case I have to kill him."

"Kill him?"

"With Baeth, you never know."

"Is this the cousin who murdered the man Eva was to marry?" Finn asked without thinking.

Dallan looked at him in askance. "She told you about that, did she?" he mused. "She hardly ever speaks of it. But yes, Baeth has never been fond of our branch of the family. He seemed to think initiating a battle and murdering Eva's betrothed would teach our Uncle Morda some sort of lesson. As far as I can tell, it only angered him further."

The muscles in Finn's jaw tightened. "If you must kill him, I will help you."

"I'm hoping it doesn't come to that, as much as I'd enjoy ridding the world of his evil. I fear our kin are so divided, retaliation would be swift for such a crime, and the last thing we need is yet another war."

Finn's opinion of Baeth was not high when they entered the feasting hall, yet somehow it managed to drop upon first sight of the man. The cavernous room lay empty except for Dallan's infamous cousin, who stood in the center by the large hearth. Half a head shorter than Finn, he was still built like a man who trained hard. His thin black hair fell about his shoulders, unkempt and unbecoming. The paleness of his pocked skin gave him the appearance of a spirit, haunting the once joyous room.

"Cousin!" he called when he noticed Dallan. He narrowed his eyes at Finn. "Who's this?"

Finn crossed his arms and glared at the bastard. Knowing he was within arm's reach of the man who caused Eva so much pain tempted him sorely. Though he wasn't about to dishonor Dallan's wishes and kill the man, he shot him a look that could not be misinterpreted.

"You didn't truly believe Brian's princes would let us meet without a third party, did you?" Dallan remarked. "Finn has no stake in politics. He is not of noble birth, and will be impartial to our discussion."

Impartial his arse. Finn would be siding with any who were against Baeth.

"He doesn't look impartial," Baeth replied skeptically, his eyes still trained on Finn.

"Why are you here, Baeth?" Dallan demanded impatiently.

"I heard you were joining Brian's Fianna, his most loyal warriors. I couldn't believe you'd betray your kin so grievously. I had to see it for myself."

"Our kin swore allegiance to Brian after the battle for Dyflin was lost," Dallan reminded him.

Baeth rolled his eyes. "You and I both know the oath was symbolic and nothing more. Sitric intends to uphold it about as much as I intend to join a monastery."

Finn's blood ran cold. If Sitric broke his oath, then—

"What about Eva?" Dallan's voice held all the rage Finn now felt. "What of my sister? Sitric would let her die for his pride?"

Baeth snorted. "Brian won't kill the girl," he waved a hand. "At most he'll have her whipped or enslaved."

Finn fought to control his breathing, feeling his nostrils flare as he contemplated how he might kill Baeth without angering Dallan or starting a blood feud.

"Brian would kill any one person if he thought it would end a rebellion," Dallan seethed. "He is a king first. He would do what was best for his kingdom."

"Spoken like a traitor," Baeth hissed.

"At least he doesn't speak like a coward," Finn spat, unable to keep out of the argument.

Baeth rounded on him. "Excuse me, boy? You dare insult me?"

"First," Finn said quietly, "no matter my age I could kill you in three moves. If you care to test that boast, by all means, draw steel.

"Second, it is no insult to speak the truth. You didn't come all this way and demand a private audience with Dallan simply to threaten his sister's wellbeing. You must be afraid to tell him why you actually came or you would've done so already."

Baeth's ruddy, bearded face soured like old milk. "When the time is ripe, I *will* kill you, whelp. And I will smile as I do so."

Dallan stepped between them. "Finn is right, and I've had enough of your foul speech. Tell me why you came or leave Cenn Cora."

Baeth's eyes never left Finn as he answered Dallan. "Sitric and I want you to turn on Brian in the upcoming battle."

Battle? Finn knew the test of bravery, the final physical trial for a place in the Fianna, must include a losing battle. Did Dallan know what they would be called to do? Was that the battle of which Baeth spoke? Or was more afoot than he imagined?

Dallan relaxed his stance, folding his arms. "Turn against him how?"

"Are you in or not? I'll not be telling you the plan until I know you'll follow it."

Dallan didn't hesitate. "I'm in, of course."

Finn's heart stopped. Was Dallan truly betraying Brian? What about becoming a *fénnid*? Rescuing Eva? He didn't want to leap to conclusions, but he had a hell of a lot of questions for Dallan when this was over.

"When he signals the charge against Mide, charge against him instead. I'll be behind you. Sitric will flank him."

Dallan nodded. "Done."

Finn hardly heard the rest of the conversation. Baeth and Dallan discussed some more details of the betrayal, then Baeth took his leave. The moment Baeth was out of the hall, Finn went after Dallan.

He opened his mouth, searching for the words to express his disappointment and concern, but Dallan headed him off.

"Obviously, I'm not going to betray Brian," he whispered, checking the doorway. "But now that I know Baeth, and possibly Sitric, will, I can ensure our forces are prepared."

Finn regarded his friend. It seemed a reasonable explanation, and up until this moment he'd never had cause to doubt Dallan. "I believe you," he allowed, "but don't you imagine Baeth will suspect your motives?"

"Of course, he does. And I never thought he'd remain loyal to Brian. I just hope that Sitric isn't truly contemplating rebellion as well. I'll need to speak with him at the battle."

Finn let out a breath he hadn't realized he'd been holding. "Would you care to tell me about this battle?"

"I'm not certain yet," Dallan admitted. "But I believe our test of bravery will be to march against Mide outnumbered, alongside my uncle's men and Sitric's."

Finn would have to digest that later. Right now, he was too busy worrying over Eva should Sitric turn against Brian. "Would Sitric really do that to Eva?" Finn asked.

Dallan sighed heavily. "I don't *think* so, but..." he shrugged. "Either way, I owe you a real explanation." He sat on the nearest bench, facing Finn with his back to the trestle table. "I knew Baeth was planning more bloodshed. I have men placed throughout Laigin and Mumhain watching him. After countless murders, I knew he was worth keeping an eye on.

"I've been trying to build up a list of evidence of his treachery to convince those of our family who support him of his ill intent. Unfortunately, that man is as slippery as an eel and as cunning as he is cruel. I've yet to gather enough witnesses to accomplish anything.

"Not long after the battle at Dyflin, Baeth uncovered one of my spies. As you might expect, he was none too pleased and started having me followed. He's always wanted me dead, since I will one day compete with him for the kingship of Laigin. I decided my best chance to expose him was to confront him. I spread word that I was coming to Cenn Cora, knowing he would follow, hoping he'd come after me and give me an opportunity to catch him."

Dallan paused, giving Finn time to absorb the tale.

"If Baeth murdered men and started battles, why wouldn't he already have incriminated himself? Why would anyone question you?"

Dallan shrugged again. "As well you know, some murder and maiming are tolerated amongst kin when battling for the throne. None have questioned him because many support him, not realizing he is more monstrous than they imagine. He will lead Leinster to destruction, not glory, with his bloodlust. Sadly not all can see this, and it is difficult to show them."

Finn didn't like that answer, but he knew Dallan told the truth. He had only one last question. "Why didn't you tell me sooner?"

"I knew when I recruited you to my aid that we would be in considerable danger once Baeth found me. I knew he would come, and I knew he'd be out for blood. Make no mistake, whether I side with him in the battle or not, he will try to kill me. I'm shocked he hasn't already made an attempt. I wanted to keep you out of this mess until I knew you could be trusted. You have been nothing but a loyal friend to me these past months. I will do all I can to repay my debt to you."

A knot formed in the pit of Finn's stomach. He needed to tell Dallan. He couldn't live his life having Dallan believe him to be some paragon when he was bedding Eva behind his back. Eva would be furious with him, he knew, but his conscience could take no more of this torment.

"Dallan," Finn began, his mouth going dry, "as we appear to be sharing secrets, there's something I need to tell you."

Dallan grinned. "Well, this I must hear."

The blood drained from Finn's face; he felt it grow colder as the full force of his betrayal struck him. Dallan smiled up at him from the bench, utterly unaware that Finn was about to shatter his world.

There was nothing for it, no turning back now.

"I'm in love with Eva."

Confusion, then disbelief, crossed his friend's countenance. The smile slipped from his face.

Finn feared it might be lost forever.

"In love?" Dallan repeated, rolling his tongue as though he were testing the words. "Terrible luck, my friend. She'll never marry, not after all she's been through."

A tragic sigh escaped Finn's lips. "I'm not sure that's true." He shifted his weight under Dallan's uncomfortable scrutiny. He didn't want to come out and say he'd bedded her, but Dallan deserved to know the extent of his betrayal.

Finn knew the moment Dallan understood his meaning.

Dallan's eyes narrowed, his voice dangerously low. "You've spent an awful lot of time alone with my sister," he growled. "Finn, if you bedded her, I swear to God—"

Finn didn't need to hear the threat. He deserved whatever justice Dallan had in mind, and he would endure it.

"I did."

# CHAPTER THIRTY

EVA COULDN'T RECALL a time when she'd been happier. She was making measurable progress on her harp skills. Her horrid cousin, Baeth, was no longer a threat to her family. And, most importantly, because she was finally safe from Baeth, she could build a life with Finn.

A glowing summer afternoon greeted her as she left her quarters for dinner in the feasting hall. She would be early, as always, to ensure all was in order before the men arrived. Before she took three steps, Cormac intercepted her.

"Well met, Lady Eva," he said, standing directly in her way.

She peeked around him, and he moved to block her again. "Is something amiss?"

"I think it best if you return to your quarters. We have an unwelcome guest near the hall." His tone gave away nothing.

"I see." It was probably related to the impending trip to Caiseal for the final trial, Eva supposed. "That's just as well. I need to speak with you anyway."

Cormac relaxed noticeably.

Apparently, he'd been expecting her to be more uncooperative. Eva didn't know if she should be flattered or insulted over that.

"I wish to accompany the men to Caiseal," she told him.

Cormac grimaced, his eyes softening. "I'm afraid I cannot allow it, Eva. Brian specifically requested that you remain here."

"Well, you see, that's the problem. I must speak with Brian.

In person."

"Is this about Finn?" he asked.

Eva took a step back, propelled by the shock of his query. "What? No. It's about Dallan." And maybe also Finn, but she wanted to keep that quiet until she spoke with Brian.

"I won't pretend to be blind to your affection for our charming bard," he told her in a gentle tone. "But I don't know that Brian will like the thought of Sitric's hostage marrying a *Fin Gall* man, Fianna or no."

Eva's pulse quickened. Had Finn told Cormac something? Or was he simply that observant? Even more concerning, were she and Finn that obvious? "Cormac," she hastened, "I don't know what you think is going on, but I assure you I mean to speak with Brian about my brother. Urgently."

She wasn't lying either. She wanted to speak with Brian about Finn, aye, but her greatest concern was her brother's freedom from hostageship. She couldn't control his acceptance to the Fianna or his willingness to join, as Finn had pointed out, but she could damn well ensure that any risk to his life wasn't on her account.

Before Cormac could respond, Dallan appeared behind him, storming toward them from the hall.

"EVA!" he shouted angrily.

Uh oh. She had no idea what he wanted, but she knew she was in trouble.

Cormac turned to stop him, but Dallan didn't slow down as he neared them.

"Eva!" he yelled again. Now that he was closer, Eva saw the fury in his face, the wildness in his eyes. "Did you, or did you not, bed Finn?"

Oh, bad.

She turned around and ran for her quarters, slamming the door just in time. A loud thud and a heavy push told her Dallan had run straight past Cormac.

"Eva! You can't ignore me forever! Answer the question!" He

banged impatiently on the small wooden door.

Eva prayed it held through his assault. She knew her brother wouldn't harm her, but she was not going to be discussing her personal life with him while he was so riled. Had Finn told him? Why would he do that? Mortification warred with righteous anger as she held fast against the quaking door.

When, after what felt an hour, the raucous ceased, Eva hoped it meant Dallan had given up and left. She opened the door a crack when it had been quiet for some time.

Dallan pushed it the rest of the way, stalking into her room, Cormac right behind him.

"Cormac," Eva pleaded, "isn't it forbidden for my brother to be speaking with me?"

Amusement flashed in Cormac's blue eyes, a much deeper shade than Finn's. "I think this warrants an exception," he replied unhelpfully. "I'll ensure you don't plot treason while you have it out with your brother."

Eva groaned in frustration.

Dallan's withering look told her she'd well and truly crossed a line. "He told me, Eva. Finn told me he bedded you. And now I want you to confirm that he told me the truth."

The intelligent move would be to deny it, but Eva's good sense fled the moment her door flew open. Instead, she voiced the first thought that came to mind. "He told you!?" she cried in disbelief. "When? Why?"

Out of the corner of her eye, she saw Cormac trying to keep from laughing. At least someone found this amusing. She certainly did not.

"Just now," Dallan answered tightly, "because, apparently, he understands the concept of guilt. Unlike a certain sister I came to rescue."

Eva narrowed her eyes. She wasn't going to roll over like some submissive pup. "I have every right to choose a lover. I only require approval for my husband."

"Do you intend to marry him?"

"I do," she ground out. Glancing at Cormac guiltily, then back to Dallan, she added, "Once I get Brian's approval."

Cormac didn't seem at all shocked by her statement.

Dallan looked murderous. Her request to marry Finn could certainly be going better.

"So I am to believe he simply told you out of nowhere, utterly unprovoked, that he was my lover?"

Dallan's horrified grimace at the word "lover" would have been amusing in a different scenario. At this moment, it only annoyed her further.

"He admitted to it after we met with Baeth," Dallan retorted. "I told him I trusted him. I thanked him for being such a good friend. He thought that was a good time to be honest with me."

Eva felt queasy. "You met with who?"

For the first time since he came after her, Dallan was speechless.

Cormac stepped forward. "He met with another noble lord, on behalf of Brian."

Eva ignored him, her eyes fixed on Dallan.

Fighting the rising panic that now threatened her. "Why was Baeth here?" she demanded. "What did he want?" Then her worst fear returned, burning brighter than a midsummer bonfire. "Does he know about Finn?" she whispered, barely able to voice the terrifying thought. "Is he after Finn?"

Tears welled but she managed not to let them spill over. God's bones, how could she have been so foolish! To think that she could finally marry. To think that Baeth was out of her life forever.

Lord, what a fool she'd been.

Dallan's face softened, his brows creasing. "No, Eva, no. He's none too pleased with Finn, but he came here to plot against Brian. Finn is safe." Dallan placed a gentle hand on her shoulder, turning to speak directly to Cormac. "We have much to discuss, though none of it surprising."

Cormac's jaw tightened, the muscles twitching. "I assumed as much. Finish up here and let's get started. Eva," he regarded her, his face kind, "I will send a messenger tomorrow for permission to grant your request." He nodded in farewell and moved to wait outside her door.

Dallan's hand fell from her shoulder. "What request?"

"I'm going to Caiseal with you," she informed him, raising her chin defiantly and pulling herself up as tall as she could manage.

"Like hell you are."

"I'm afraid that's up to the king, not you," she reminded him tartly, praying he left before she fell to pieces entirely. "Now go tell Cormac all about our horrid cousin and leave me be."

Dallan backed away, frowning. "Don't think for a moment we're through discussing this marriage business. As I no longer trust Finn, I'm reluctant to give him permission to marry my sister."

"Just go." Eva shooed him out the door in a final, desperate grasp at solitude.

The moment the door shut, she collapsed in tears onto her bed. It didn't matter if Dallan gave his approval or not.

Now that Baeth had returned, she wouldn't be marrying Finn anyway.

# CHAPTER THIRTY-ONE

AFTER DINNER THAT evening, Finn paced in front of the alcove where he and Eva met for their nightly lessons in the great hall. He could hardly blame her if she didn't want to meet, but he desperately hoped she would at least be willing to speak with him.

He had missed her conversation with Dallan, who had punched him squarely on the jaw before ordering Finn not to follow him out of the hall after Finn's sensational admission. He'd rather hoped to feel less guilty after a good hit, but it did nothing to ease his conscience. And, as far as he could tell, it did little to lessen Dallan's anger with him either.

At dinner, Dallan hadn't spoken a word to him. Diarmid and Conan attempted, but failed, to pry any information from Dallan about his foul mood. Finn wasn't about to tell them anything that Dallan didn't want to share. Instead, Finn had spent all of his meal contemplating how to make things right with both Dallan and Eva.

He knew Eva would be upset, but he hoped the damage was reparable. Knowing her, she'd probably be furious with Dallan and disappointed that Finn had told him before they agreed. They both knew Dallan would be upset either way. Eva had simply hoped to lessen the shock.

Even after finishing the last bite of his meal, Finn still had no idea how to make things right with Dallan. He knew he'd need time, and he supposed he'd need to confront him again, but what would he say?

Finn breathed a sigh of relief when Eva walked over to him in the alcove after dinner. "I was worried you wouldn't come," he admitted quietly.

"I certainly considered it." She sat down in one of the two wooden chairs, smoothing her pale blue skirt over her knees. She hadn't brought her harp.

"I'm sorry." Finn decided there was no point in dancing around the issue. "I know we agreed to wait to tell Dallan, but I just couldn't keep lying to him. I'm sorry that I didn't give you any warning."

Eva glanced toward the tables, frowning, her lips pursed.

Finn followed her gaze to find Dallan glaring at them. When Finn looked at him, he stood abruptly and left the hall.

"Do you think he'll forgive me?" he asked Eva, not sure he wanted to hear the answer.

"I honestly don't know," she replied. "He's always had a bit of a temper and tended toward the dramatic, but I've never seen him so upset. I think you were right to tell him, Finn. I don't blame you for doing so."

Finn nodded, swallowing. He'd already made so many mistakes, disappointed so many people. He feared he'd do so again. But it was too late. He was in too deep. So he spoke the words he'd held in his heart since the moment he told Dallan their secret.

"I love you," Finn whispered, kneeling before her so that his face was level with hers. He cradled one of her delicate hands between both his own. "I will do whatever I must to be with you, and to make amends with your brother. If you wish it, I will stay here with you. I will leave the trials. I will beg Dallan for permission. I will be yours alone."

"Finn," Eva breathed.

Finn didn't like the look on her face, so he kept going, hoping. "Will you still marry me?"

A single tear trickled down her cheek, a glittering path in its wake. "No."

He took a step backward, rising as he moved away from her. "But, why? It was only last night that you told me—"

"I know what I told you last night," Eva interrupted, her voice breaking. "And I retract it. We cannot be together. I won't be needing any further lessons."

Finn felt as though he'd been hit by a galloping horse, knocked flat on his back, struggling to draw breath. He stood as still as a stone, unable to accept her harsh dismissal. "Will you not even tell me why?" he repeated. "Is it because of your cousin? You know I am capable of defending both of us."

Eva stood. "It doesn't matter the issue. It cannot be remedied." She walked past him, turning before she was to the nearest table. "Goodbye, Finn. I am grateful for the time we shared, truly. And I wish you only the best."

ON THE MORN of the trial of recovery, Finn contemplated giving up entirely. Dawn broke early, purple wisps of cloud woven through a pink and orange horizon. For the first time since he arrived at Cenn Cora, Dallan didn't come to his tent before walking up to the training field.

For the first time since he arrived at Cenn Cora, he didn't know what to do next. He considered leaving, admitting it had been a fool's quest from the start and returning home broken and alone. But then he remembered Ethlinn. He remembered that his family would have no recourse for justice if he didn't make something of himself. He hoped Eva would still help Eth, but Finn needed his own plan as well. He'd not been able to join the ranks of the bardic masters, but this he could do. He could become one of the Fianna. He was already so close, to give up now would be to throw away all that he had endured.

Eva had shattered his heart, broken his spirit. What bothered him the most was her refusal to give him a reason. He would have understood had it been her cousin's presence in Cenn Cora, returning to her life seemingly out of nowhere.

But she'd denied Baeth's presence as the problem. Something that deeply unsettled Finn. Perhaps he'd been more wrong about her than he could have imagined.

Perhaps she'd never truly intended to marry.

She was the one person who knew all his secrets, who knew more about him than anyone else. He thought she accepted him, in spite of his heritage. In spite of his failures and shortcomings.

Now he wasn't so certain.

Initially, he thought she was simply rejecting a betrothal. But, after giving it far too much thought, Finn realized Eva wasn't rejecting a betrothal. She was rejecting *him*.

His mood as dark as the sun was bright, Finn joined the rest of the men for their final trial at Cenn Cora.

This particular trial wasn't one that the residents of the keep and village could watch. Of course, many of them came anyway, but it was nigh impossible to track a man as he ran up and down the hill.

The fourteen men who remained lined up before the trees. One at a time, they ran down the hillside and up again through the dense forest. Cormac and Broccan took turns chasing them, ensuring they never slowed and that they removed the thorns they stepped on as they went. Upon their return to the top of the hill, the bottoms of their feet were inspected to be certain they hadn't feigned the injury.

Finn took a place near the center of the line, next to a grim-looking Dallan.

"You'll do just fine," Finn told him, as though they were still friends. For Finn's part, that had never changed.

Dallan ignored him.

"What in God's name is going on with you two?" Diarmid asked from Dallan's other side. Conan, next to him and the furthest from Finn, leaned forward curiously. "It's like watching a lovers' quarrel."

"Why don't you ask Finn?" Dallan muttered, never breaking his blank stare toward the forest.

Diarmid shot Finn a pointed look, eyes wide.

Finn looked at his feet, grimacing, determined to cooperate. "I may have bedded his sister."

Diarmid nearly choked on his laughter.

Conan's mouth fell so far open he could have caught a bird in it. "You did not!"

"Not helpful," Dallan growled.

When Diarmid's laughter faded and he was once more capable of speech, he shook his head at Finn. "I'm guessing you didn't ask Dallan about it first, eh? You broke one of the only rules of friendship."

"I didn't mean to," Finn defended, unthinking. "It just sort of—happened."

"It always does," Diarmid agreed, a little too cheerily for Finn's liking. "It always does."

Cormac called the first man to the woods, giving chase seconds behind him.

"You'll have to talk to him eventually, Dallan," Conan said. "You're both going to end up as Fianna, and you know it. You can't see each other every day and never speak to him."

"I certainly can," Dallan argued.

Something about Dallan's tone sparked a fire in Finn. "You can't," he countered. "And I'm going to follow you every day until you finally talk to me about this."

Broccan and the second man, Ardál, disappeared into the forest. Cormac and the first man returned, stopping immediately to inspect the runner's feet.

"Fine!" Dallan rounded on him, arms folded defiantly. "You want to talk about it, let's talk about it. You lied to me. You violated my sister. You betrayed our friendship, my trust. Am I forgetting anything?"

"Conan!" Cormac called. "Get your hairy arse over here!"

Conan raised his eyebrows before running into the woods for his trial, his elder brother on his heels.

"Yes, as a matter of fact, you are." Finn didn't know what the hell he was thinking, but he couldn't stop once he began. The words tumbled out like water from a broken dam. "I *didn't* violate your sister. I love her. And I'm going to marry her."

Dallan snorted, his face turning red. "I'm not letting you anywhere near her, and I'm certainly not agreeing to a betrothal. Not to someone like you."

Broccan called out, and Diarmid took off for his turn through the woods.

Finn had had enough. "You see! This is why I didn't tell you sooner! I wanted to so many times, to tell you how much I love her, how wonderful she is, but I knew—*I knew*—you'd never approve of the match. Of course, the niece of a king can't marry the son of an Ostman farmer."

All the fire left Dallan's face, leaving behind a look of disappointment that crushed Finn. "You want to know the truth, Finn?"

Cormac returned. "Dallan! You're up!"

Dallan took a step out of line toward Cormac, but turned around, pausing. "I would have given her to you, gladly, if you had asked me. I don't care who you are or what your parents do for a living. If you make my sister happy, that's enough for me. You're the best man I know."

"Dallan!"

"Or I thought you were."

Finn watched as Dallan disappeared into the forest, followed by Cormac. Dallan's words played over and over in his mind. *I would have given her to you. You're the best man I know.*

*Or I thought you were.*

As Broccan returned to call Finn for his turn, the reality of his mistake settled deep in his gut.

Dallan may never forgive him.

# CHAPTER THIRTY-TWO

TWO DAYS LATER, Eva rode in the center of the men as they climbed the hillside to Caiseal, grateful that the king had agreed to her request. Much like Cenn Cora, the seat of the kings of Mumhain overlooked the nearby countryside from a lofty perch, ideal for defending. Instead of a forest, however, a patchwork blanket of fields covered the land around the fortress.

It had taken every ounce of self-control not to look at the men who rode around her. Now, as they reined in the horses and slowed to dismount, Eva knew she must finally face the object of her thoughts over the past days. Stepping down from her steady mare, she looked around, taking in her new surroundings.

With a will of their own, her eyes landed on Finn. Her chest ached as she watched him dismount, his sand-colored hair reminding her of all the nights they'd spent together on the shores of Loch Derg.

For the briefest moment, his eyes met hers. As soon as he registered her attention, he looked away.

If only Finn hated her. It would be so much easier to bear than the pain she saw on his face. She knew she'd hurt him.

She also knew that if she'd told him the truth—that Baeth *was* the reason she called off the betrothal—that he would go after her cousin. She thought she had been ready, she truly believed she wasn't afraid of him anymore. But that was when she thought he would be out of her life forever. Having him appear not just in her life, but ten paces from her quarters, served as a stark reminder of what was at stake. She no longer clung to such childish fantasies.

She had always known that no one she loved would be safe. She was a fool to have forgotten as much. At least she remembered before Finn had to pay for her poor decisions with his life.

Did she believe Finn could defeat Baeth? Aye, she thought he stood a fair chance.

Was she willing to wager his life on it? Never.

She couldn't save Dallan from her cousin's bloodlust. He had been born to it. But she could save Finn.

The rest of the men dismounted around them. After the Trial of Recovery, eleven men accompanied Cormac and Broccan to Caiseal to complete the most dangerous trial: the Trial of Bravery. As Eva understood it, the men had to charge to certain death without losing their courage. She thought that sounded more foolhardy than brave, but then again she was no *fénnid*. Perhaps there was more to it than that.

To her displeasure, Dallan had passed the trial. She wasn't terribly surprised; she knew her brother had performed well at the trials thus far. But after Finn told her he was struggling, she'd held out hope that perhaps the problem would fix itself.

So now she had the pleasure of spending the day fretting over both her brother *and* the man she loved.

Brian and Dunla, his much younger, statuesque queen, descended a small staircase in the center of the courtyard. Dunla was Brian's third wife, not even ten summers Eva's senior. Quiet and biddable, with an easy smile and locks so dark a raven would be envious, she was the pinnacle of grace and poise. An easy choice for an aging king.

Dunla nodded kindly toward Eva, but Brian did not even acknowledge her. She could hardly be insulted. She was only a hostage, after all, and the bad blood between their families went back many years.

"Cormac, Broccan," the king greeted his men, "it's good to have you home. Come, we have much to discuss. Bring the men."

Cormac and Broccan both stepped forward, the former embracing the queen without the slightest hesitation. Conan and Diarmid hurried to join, all four of them grinning like fools.

"You can spend time with your sister once we've finished our meeting," Brian grumbled.

Eva managed to keep her mouth from falling agape at that statement. How had she not realized that the queen was their sister? Before she could properly inspect the siblings for a family resemblance, they all disappeared into the hall.

And just like that, Eva was alone.

DINNER CAME AND went, and Eva began to lose hope that she would have an audience with the king before he rode to battle the following morn. Sitting in a chair before the great hearth in the center of the feasting hall, Eva stared into the dancing flames. She still had to convince Cormac to allow her to speak with her brother, as well.

Pain struck her like lightning whenever she thought of Finn going to battle, but she couldn't say goodbye to him. She'd already done it and seeing him again would only weaken her resolve.

"Eva?" As though summoned by her musings, Cormac appeared before her. "The king will see you now."

Eva stood, following him away from the fire's warm light. "Will you let me speak with Dallan tonight?" she asked. "Before the battle?"

Cormac stopped walking and turned to face her. "Of course," he answered softly. "I'm no monster. You can farewell your brother." He paused, searching her expression. "I can point you toward Finn as well."

Another wrenching pain seared through Eva's chest. Would it ever end? Or would she feel this every time she thought of him? "Thank you," she choked out, "but I only need to speak with my brother."

He raised an eyebrow but said nothing. He didn't need to voice his thoughts—they were written plainly on his face.

"It's for the best," Eva assured herself more than Cormac.

"As you wish."

He led her across the courtyard to the expansive stone solar, newly constructed, that held the royal family's private chambers. The sun hung low in the western sky, but yet lay in sight. Cormac opened the door for her, following her in and guiding her to Brian's solar.

She'd only been in the room a handful of times since becoming a hostage. Unlike the modest solar in Cenn Cora, the chamber in Caiseal normally glowed with radiant light from two walls of windows. Tonight, those windows were shuttered.

A log popped and hissed in the hearth along the far wall, flanked by four exquisite chairs. Books and parchments lined two shelves on either side of the fire, a testament to Brian's education and wealth. The man himself, who held her life in his hands, reclined in a chair sipping ale.

Cormac gave Eva a gentle push into the room before closing the door behind her.

"Come," Brian called without turning around. "Sit."

Eva did as he bid her, sitting in the chair nearest the door and furthest from Brian. She folded her hands in her lap uncomfortably, feeling very much on display.

"Cormac tells me you're displeased with the deal I made with your brother."

"I am." If he was going to get right to it, so would she. "Sitric and my uncle offered me as the hostage because it makes the most sense. I have come to beg you to uphold the original agreement."

"Would it not make more sense for me to take away a potential heir to the throne of my enemy?"

Eva caught Brian's eye. "Laigin is no longer your enemy. Morda swore allegiance to you. He offered me in the agreement as a surety. Would it not make more sense to uphold that agreement? It seems to me that if you dismiss me as a hostage, my family might see it as an opening for rebellion, a breaking of the agreement."

The hint of a smile played at the corner of his wrinkled lips. "For a quiet thing, you're certainly clever," he chuckled. "You make a fair point, but you know, perhaps even more than I, the odds of rebellion by your family are high no matter your status as a hostage."

Eva's heart sank. She watched him take a long sip of ale, wondering if all her hopes were fading before her eyes. His grey beard glowed a brilliant orange in the flickering firelight.

"Why?" he asked. "Why are you so against your brother taking your place?"

"Because I love him," Eva replied simply. "Sitric asked me to be his hostage offering, he let me decide. I agreed to spare those I love from such a burden. My brother, even if he never becomes king, he will marry. He will have children. As will Astrid. I gave up on such dreams long ago." Her voice broke over her last words. "I am the one who is giving up nothing."

Brian watched her for several uncomfortable breaths, taking in her measure. "I believe you."

Eva let out a breath.

"And, though I don't trust your family as far as I can throw a stone, you are correct that they will rebel sooner if I dismantle our agreement."

Hope, after so many days of despair, lifted her spirits.

"I will grant your request. It is nobly done and makes sense for my aims and my kingdom."

"Oh, thank you!" She managed to stop herself from jumping out of her chair, but only just.

He dismissed her with a wave of his hand and a sip of his ale, staring once again into the dancing flames.

She'd done it! She'd actually done it. Her brother's future was secured. He could live his life, and she could sacrifice hers, just as she'd planned. His ruin wouldn't be on her head. She should feel elated, positively joyful.

So why, as she followed Cormac back out of the solar com-plex, did Eva feel so empty?

# CHAPTER THIRTY-THREE

CORMAC LED EVA just outside the keep's palisade to the base of the hill, where eleven tents stood in orderly rows. Smoke rose from the small fire ring, dancing in the warm evening breeze, blissfully unaware of the gravity of the night. Three men sat around the fire, Dallan among them.

As Eva and Cormac approached, he looked up and stood to meet them, his face unreadable.

Eva stood several paces from her brother, just staring at him. He had always been there for her, from her earliest memories to the day she became a hostage. Dallan had never stopped protecting her.

This time, she could protect him instead.

"You don't have to go," she whispered. "I've spoken with Brian, and he has agreed to uphold the original hostage agreement made by Sitric."

Dallan's fists tightened, his arms crossing his chest. "He didn't," Dallan countered. "He wouldn't go back on his word."

"If I may," Cormac interrupted, "Eva is correct. He will uphold the original bargain, thereby not going back on his word to Sitric."

"Eva," her brother's voice broke with emotion, "why will you not let me protect you? Why must you be so difficult?"

"I won't have anyone risking their life for me. By death or by imprisonment, it does not matter. I chose to act as Sitric's hostage, and I will see it through. Now please, I beg you, leave before the battle. Live the life that was meant for you."

Dallan walked within arms' reach, his voice quiet, his gaze unwavering. "*This* is the life that was meant for me. To fight on behalf of a king until I become one myself, should I be so unlucky. I will not abandon them now, on the eve of a battle when I am needed most."

A lump formed in Eva's chest, making it difficult to think straight. All her begging, all her efforts with Brian, and she still might lose her brother tomorrow. "Is there naught I can say to sway you?"

"My mind is made." He shifted his weight uncomfortably. "And, as I may not return, we should probably speak of Finn and your future."

"Aye," Eva agreed, steeling herself for battle of a different sort, "we should."

Dallan opened his mouth to begin the discussion, but Eva cut him off.

"You need not worry over it any longer. I will not be marrying him," she choked out the words, ignoring the stinging in her eyes. "I will not be marrying anyone."

"Eva," he warned, "as much as I dislike Finn, you cannot throw away your life over fear of one man."

Her resolve wavered at the mention of Baeth, bile rising from deep in her belly. But she would not put Finn at risk. Instead, she would do what she could to mend his friendship with Dallan before the morn. "Just as you cannot throw away your friendship over one slight."

"That's not the same at all," he grumbled.

"It is," Eva pressed. "You will never forgive yourself if you march into battle and lose him tomorrow without making peace."

Dallan's pained expression told her his answer before he spoke a word. "I cannot," he sighed. "I yet feel the sting of his betrayal."

"You won't forever," Eva warned. "And when one day, maybe years from now, you realize how small his offense truly was, you will forever regret losing such a dear friend over it."

"Then that is a sin I shall have to live with."

Eva shook her head, huffing at her brother's obstinance. "Finn helped you when you asked it of him. He followed you here without question, ready to walk into danger if necessary. The only misstep he took was listening to me instead of you, when I begged him to keep our feelings for one another secret. Finn wanted to tell you from the beginning. *I* convinced him to wait. Do not blame him for my poor judgment."

Dallan's brows knitted, barely perceptible in the mantle of darkness now surrounding them. Whatever thoughts crossed his mind after her declaration, he kept to himself. When it was clear he had nothing more to say on the matter, Eva pulled him into an embrace.

"Be safe, dear brother," she whispered into his chest.

He kissed the top of her head tenderly. "Fear not. I will return."

Eva made haste away from the encampment, lest she be tempted to seek out Finn as well. The ache in her chest threatened to overcome her good sense if she didn't hurry. She thanked Cormac before retreating to her own modest quarters.

Come the morn, she could lose the two people who mattered most—Dallan and Finn. How could she possibly sleep? How could she do anything except worry? Her deepest fears creeping in from the shadows of her heart, Eva did the only thing she could manage.

She reached for her harp.

Hours later, as dawn broke over the eastern horizon, the final chords of her song, the Song of the Fianna, fled on a westerly breeze.

FINN REFUSED TO give in to despair completely. His heart was wracked over the guilt of betraying his best friend and the ache of losing the woman he loved.

Belting on his scabbard, he stepped into the crisp air of daybreak. One by one, the other men joined him in silence. No one jested this morn; every man knew it might be his last. Dallan emerged, his face grim. He nodded at Diarmid and Conan, ignoring Finn entirely. As one, the eleven men walked up the hillside to the courtyard.

Brian sat on his white stallion, a crown of gold about his brow. His sons, Murrough and Tadc flanked him on their own steeds. Cormac and Broccan took their positions behind him. Like the rest of the men, they went on foot. Queen Dunla stood atop the staircase leading to the feasting hall, resplendent in a blue and gold léine to match the king's.

Finn's breath caught when he spotted Eva, standing in the doorway to her quarters on his other side. Her eyes cast down, her chestnut hair plaited tightly down her back. Boring into her with his eyes, he prayed to all the gods that she would feel his gaze and look up at him one last time.

She didn't.

When Brian spurred his horse to begin the march, Finn realized he had lost her forever.

# CHAPTER THIRTY-FOUR

T HEY RODE FOR over three days, reaching Nás, the seat of the kings of Laigin, just before midday on the fourth day. Finn looked to Dallan, wishing his friend would speak with him. He'd love to hear Dallan's thoughts on returning to his ancestral home as part of another king's retinue.

Stopping only long enough to sleep and eat a small meal, they continued the march toward Mide, now joined by Dallan's uncle, King Morda of Leinster, and his cousin, King Sitric of Dyflin. Dallan shared features with his uncle but could not look more different than Sitric. Sitting tall atop his speckled stallion, this man, who had become something of a mythical figure to Finn, stood apart from all other men. Just as all aspects of Brian's appearance cried out as echoes of his ancient forefathers, so, too, did Sitric embody all that Finn associated with the homeland of his father's kin.

His golden hair, near the color of Finn's own, fell to his shoulders, braided here and there with golden beads. His beard was shorter than Finn expected, particularly for a man nicknamed 'Silkbeard,' but was impressive all the same. A deep crimson cloak flowed behind him, draping both horse and rider in the rich, blood-red fabric. The golden trim on his snow-white tunic showcased his immense wealth. Unlike the natives of Éire, Finn's kinsmen from the north wore armor into battle. Sitric wore a shirt of mail rings over his chest and leather bracers on his forearms.

When Sitric caught sight of Dallan, he fell into step with him, dismounting and walking beside him.

"Cousin!" he bellowed, holding his horse's reins in one hand and smacking the breath out of Dallan with the other.

Finn barely concealed a laugh at the vivacity of this man he'd heard so much about over the past months. From Eva.

His heart lurched in pain at the thought. How she'd love to be here, to see her uncle and cousin again. If she ever spoke with him again, Finn would tell her all about her cousin's antics.

As if realizing he watched them, Dallan and Sitric both turned to look at Finn. Dallan glared at him. Sitric attacked him with an utterly disarming smile before narrowing his eyes. Finn pitied the lady who was on the receiving end of such charm.

The following day, marching in the same order, Cormac appeared at his side while Finn watched Sitric and Dallan.

"I thought you might appreciate knowing our plan before charging into battle," he remarked casually.

Finn looked at the modest size of their force—no more than two hundred men altogether—and sighed. "Whatever it is, let's hope we have enough men. Or they don't."

Cormac's lips thinned. "We don't have enough men," he replied. "That is the test."

"Brian is willing to throw away two hundred men for a battle he knows he'll likely lose?" Finn asked incredulously. "Wouldn't it be better to simply send the Fianna in and reserve his allies' forces for a more favorable encounter?"

Cormac leaned closer, so that no one else could overhear his reply. "The Fianna are not the only ones being tested this day."

Understanding dawned, followed quickly by resignation. So, Brian tested the bravery of the Fianna and the loyalty of his new suppliants in one. If Finn's fate was to die in battle, surely it would be this one. He hadn't much faith in the latter's loyalty.

"We will arrive at the southern border of Mag Bregh by midafternoon. Their scouts will have seen us, and their army will be waiting. We'll be lucky to reach the Hill of Tara. Sitric and

Morda will lead the charge, as they are entirely cavalry. The Fianna will follow on foot. We will lose, almost certainly, but we will fight until Brian calls for retreat. If you make it that long, you will have proven your bravery and will be a *fénnid* in all but oath."

"And what of Baeth's planned betrayal," Finn hissed under breath, shooting a glare toward the bastard.

"We expect it, and have additional men guarding the king, but we don't have enough information to do much else. All the men are to keep watch for signs of treachery."

Finn didn't like that answer, but he knew Cormac must feel similarly. After all, their fearless leader had a strong fosterage bond with Brian. He and Broccan, more than any of them, would be invested in protecting the king.

Cormac took his leave, moving to the next warrior to have a similar conversation, and Finn once more observed the men who had come with Laigin and Dyflin. Turning around, he noticed for the first time that Dallan's cousin, Baeth, rode on the Fianna's flank, watching Sitric and Dallan. A contingent of around twenty or so men rode with him, set visibly apart from the rest of the Laigin forces.

Had Dallan noticed him yet? Finn thought not, as his friend hadn't looked behind them at all. Dallan had known he would be here, knew he plotted treachery, yet seemed amazingly unconcerned over it.

"He'll get over it, eventually." Diarmid's low statement interrupted his thoughts. "If we all survive the battle, that is."

"Is there aught I can do?" Finn asked, hoping Diarmid knew something he didn't. "Anything to make it up to him?"

Diarmid shook his head. "Just give him some time. He'll come 'round'."

"How are your nerves?" Finn changed the subject, no longer able to stomach a conversation of his ruined friendship.

Diarmid grinned. "Unwavering, as always."

Before Finn could reply, Brian held up a fist, calling for a halt. In front of him to the left, Sitric mounted and rode to join the

King of Mumhain. Baeth followed close on his heels.

Finn looked up and saw that as he spoke with Diarmid they'd at last come in sight of the ancient seat of the High Kings of Éire: Tara. An unsettling feeling descended upon Finn as he stood before it, recalling how hundreds of years earlier the Fianna, led by Finn mac Cumhail, had suffered their greatest defeat in this very spot. Surely, that did not bode well for today's battle. Finn couldn't help but wonder if that legend had been part of Brian's planning of this trial.

It stood upon an enormous hill, wider than Caiseal and taller than Cenn Cora, its wooden palisade high enough to obscure the buildings that lay within.

At the base of the grass-covered hill, an army several-hundred-strong awaited them.

The hollow clang of spear hitting shield rang across the valley as the men of Mide taunted the invaders. With no ceremony whatsoever, Brian signaled the charge.

He had been so busy worrying over Dallan and Eva and talking with Cormac and Diarmid that Finn hadn't given the battle much consideration. Until the moment he drew steel and charged headlong into it.

Heart pounding, determination shooting like lightning through his veins, Finn ran.

Dallan before him.

Diarmid and Conan beside him.

Sitric so far ahead that only his red cloak remained visible, flapping like a harbinger of death behind him. The horsemen of Laigin and Dyflin pierced the lines of Mide from either side, pinching them into a tighter formation and surrounding them from three sides against the hill.

Finn followed Dallan straight into the front line, ignoring the whooshing in his ears as his sword fell for the first time.

He'd fought before, aye, but never in a true battle. At this moment, it was best to forget that fact.

He cut down men as he waded deeper into the fray. One.

Two. Three men down, a fourth quick to follow. In a brief moment of respite, he turned to check on his friends.

Diarmid and Conan battled back-to-back, as did Cormac and Broccan. Dallan spun in circles, defending himself on all sides.

"Stubborn bastard," Finn muttered, sprinting to help his friend. If Dallan kept up that pace, he'd tire too quickly.

Panting hard, Dallan nodded to Finn in acknowledgement before turning to fight the next spearman. Back-to-back they fought, wave after wave of warriors crashing against their skillful defense.

All thought fled Finn. He slashed. He blocked. He side-stepped. His sword became an extension of his being, the only thing keeping him from a gruesome death. His body moved with the memory of years of practice, preparing him for this moment.

After slaying his opponent innumerable, Finn looked up, letting his head fall back as the sun beat down on his sweat-covered brow. He couldn't take much more before exhaustion overcame his resolve. At least he'd been able to help Dallan before they both tired.

Shouting across the field drew his attention. A group of riders had broken away from the battle, turning tail and galloping back toward the king and his guard. Squinting, Finn realized with horror that Baeth led the retreat.

Except it wasn't a retreat.

It was an attack on the king.

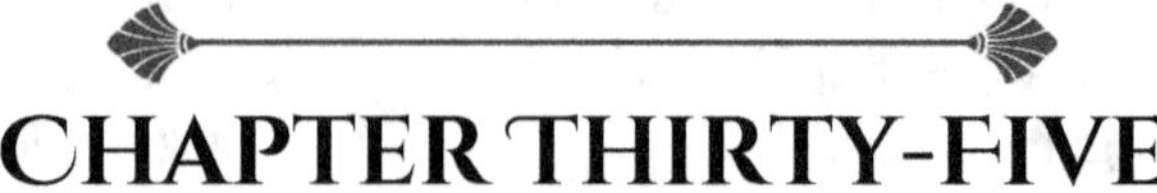

# CHAPTER THIRTY-FIVE

"Cormac!" Finn shouted, grabbing Dallan's shirtsleeve and yanking him to their commanders. "Cormac! To the king!"

Upon hearing his cry, Dallan looked toward Brian, swearing a volatile oath and taking off on his own, doing his damndest to chase down twenty horsemen.

Calling once more for Cormac, Finn sprinted after him. He wasn't about to let Dallan fight Baeth alone.

Baeth's men reached the king when Dallan and Finn were halfway across the field. Brian drew his sword, his guard taking up his defense while Dallan and Finn closed the distance.

Finn's fury welled up from deep in his belly, burning hotter than a smith's forge. He was going to kill Baeth. After all he'd done to Eva, after the threat he posed to first Dallan and now the king, Finn wouldn't let him leave this battlefield alive.

Cormac, at a full run on a stolen horse, passed them as they went, entering the fray with a roar of anger. He'd better not get to Baeth first. The only way Finn could let the killing blow pass is if Dallan landed it himself.

His sword moved with a will of its own, cutting a path alongside Dallan directly for Baeth.

Four horsemen toward the back noticed them, turning to charge. Finn and Dallan sidestepped the charge in opposite directions, separated from one another with half the horsemen between them.

"Baeth!" Finn shouted, continuing to move lest he be trampled by one of the horses. Screams and steel surrounded him, a dizzying cacophony of violence.

Behind him, Finn heard Diarmid, Conan, and Broccan, as well as the shouts of several other men. All of them worked to cut a path to Brian.

Sunlight glinted off a sword out of the corner of his eye. Finn turned, springing into action. Baeth had reached Brian.

Finn's breath caught as Baeth's sword hit Brian's horse, narrowly missing the king. He wouldn't make it in time.

But Dallan did.

Brian dismounted before the horse fell upon him as Dallan moved to defend the king from Baeth. Finn neared them, watching as they dueled. For several strokes, Dallan had the advantage. He beat Baeth back with hit after hit.

Then Baeth's men noticed the duel.

Abandoning their own fights, they descended on Dallan and the king with devastating force. Cormac reached the king in time to defend him alongside the guardsmen, working to free him from the melee.

Brian called for a retreat. All the Fianna in sight ran after him, protecting their king and their own backs.

All the Fianna, except Dallan.

Finn watched as his best friend was swallowed whole by a dozen men, many still mounted. Baeth gained the upper hand before Dallan disappeared from sight.

He didn't hesitate a moment. His friend needed him. Finn roared, drawing as much attention away from Dallan as he could. He cut down two men, forcing his way to Dallan within the circle.

Covered in blood but still fighting, Dallan spun with the ferocity of a caged wolf, his sword flying from one man to the next.

While Dallan turned his attention to a horseman spearing him from behind, Baeth lifted his sword to take advantage of the opening.

Finn's shield caught the blow. Relief washed over him. He'd made it just in time.

Baeth's skill with the sword challenged Finn, but Finn's simmering rage gave him an edge. As Dallan returned to join in the fight against Baeth, Finn's sword slid into his chest.

The thundering of hooves preceded a flank attack by Sitric, who grinned like a fool as he and his men dispatched the last of the traitors.

"Mide is coming!" he called to Dallan and Finn, urging his mount to follow after Brian and the Fianna.

They ran several miles before finally leaving the enemy warriors behind, every man dropping to the ground or doubling over to catch his breath.

Except Dallan.

"You're a relentless bastard, you know that?" Dallan yelled, stalking toward him, tossing his shield on the grass. "I was determined, unwaveringly determined to loathe you for the rest of eternity." He reached Finn, dropping his sword and pulling him into an embrace. "And then you had to go and save my life, you heathen."

When Dallan released him, Finn saw the raw emotion contorting his features.

"Whether you loathe me or not, I will always have your back in a battle. To you, I will always be a friend."

Dallan's brow furrowed deeply, his eyes thoughtful. "I believe today you have proven as much," he agreed, offering his forearm to Finn.

He grasped it in return, smiling for the first time in days. At least he had Dallan back.

"About my sister," Dallan began, narrowing his eyes, "I've given it much thought since we left Nás this morning. And though I'm not overly fond of being kept in the dark over it, I think I was meant to find you. For Eva. I've never seen her so happy as when she had you."

Another bolt of pain struck Finn's chest. "I'm afraid it doesn't matter," he sighed. "She won't even look at me, let alone speak with me."

"Baeth is gone," Dallan reminded him. "You've won the right to her. She feared his wrath, and now she is freed of it. Once she learns of his death she'll feel differently."

"I'm not sure she will," Finn replied heavily. "Baeth was the figurehead of her fears. I think they run more deeply than even his offenses."

"She spoke to me on your behalf. Last night after supper."

The faintest glimmer of hope flickered to life from the dying coals. "She did?"

"Aye," Dallan told him, folding his arms, "and though she tried to hide it, I could see that she wished to seek you out. She fought for you, told me everything was her own fault and I ought to forgive you."

Finn's stomach flipped. "Do you think it will be enough?" he asked, allowing himself to wonder. "If Baeth is gone, will she let go of her fear?"

Dallan let a heavy hand fall upon Finn's shoulder. "There's only one way to find out."

# CHAPTER THIRTY-SIX

Eva felt like the waking dead, a ghost haunting the hillside around Caiseal. She had slept but fitfully since the night she spoke with Dallan, a fortnight ago now. They should be returning—the march in total would only take twelve or thirteen days and the battle one or two at most. They could be back any day now.

She paced, her thoughts flitting through her mind like birds refusing a cage. What if Finn died? What if Dallan died? What if neither returned? Finally, sitting in a huff on the steps of the hall, Eva let her head fall in her hands.

Her fear for the men she loved was enough to undo her. Dallan and Finn risked their lives for Brian, and what could she do about it?

Not a damned thing.

Maybe Dallan had been right. Maybe her fear served no purpose but to torment her.

With resolve she didn't know dwelt within her, Eva stood. She couldn't help Dallan. She couldn't help Finn. They'd both gone to battle for their own purposes.

Maybe it was time Eva stopped blaming herself for their actions.

Stepping into her quarters only long enough to grab her harp, Eva walked down the hillside to the nearest forest. She was done waiting in fear.

SOME HOURS LATER, as the sun teased the western horizon until it reddened, Eva heard commotion up in the fortress.

All her thoughts of waiting patiently fled. Excitement, hope, and, of course, fear bubbled within her belly like an untended cauldron. Eva raced back up the hill, harp in hand.

Only to find the courtyard empty. She spotted Queen Dunla on her way to the hall and rushed to intercept her.

"Are they back?" she asked breathlessly, not caring how out of sorts she sounded.

Dunla smiled brightly. "Yes," she replied. "We're preparing a feast now. Luckily, the kitchen expected one soon. The men have gone off with Brian to get cleaned up and memorize their oaths. Dinner will be in an hour, just after sunset."

Excitement trickled through Eva. "Did Dallan come back? Finn?"

"Both are here."

Eva took a step backward, absorbing the queen's words. They both lived. They both came back. Her eyes stung with tears, pinpricks threatening to unleash a storm at any moment. Lord, she couldn't be happier.

Dunla gave her a supportive smile. "Why don't you go ready yourself?" she suggested, giving Eva a small push toward her quarters. "We'll expect you in an hour for the ceremony."

One hour felt like ten as Eva donned her cream-colored gown and let her hair down, taming it into loose waves that reached her hips. She only hoped Finn would meet with her after dinner, so she could beg him to reconsider marriage.

She'd figure out how to get Dallan to agree later. Right now, she needed to get Finn back.


EVA ENTERED THE hall, trepidation in every step. Torches flickered along the edge of the walls. A hearth roared in the center before the dais, its flames fighting their confines, licking excitedly at the stone rim. A boar roasted on a spit over the hearth, its succulent, rich scent filling the room and making Eva's stomach grumble.

Rows of trestle tables held a hundred or more folk from the village. Upon the dais, Brian stood in the center with Dunla to his right. Cormac and Broccan stood to his left. When Eva looked beside Broccan, she finally lost the battle for her composure.

"Sitric!" she cried, hurrying to the dais to embrace her beloved cousin. "What are you doing here?"

Sitric grinned down at her, his eyes glinting in the firelight. "Brian and I have some business to attend to following the battle," he told her. "And I couldn't pass up the opportunity to visit my favorite cousin." He winked at her, placing a gentle kiss on her forehead, before she returned to her table.

Taking her seat at the base of the dais, her heart fuller than she had thought possible, she could hardly wait to speak with Sitric. To hear news of Astrid, of Aunt Gormla. To relax into the familiar.

The doors opened then, and five men entered, all wearing green cloaks and brown léine. All looking battle-worn. Cormac's younger brothers, Conan and Diarmid, entered first, followed by a man she knew as Ardál. Finn and Dallan came through last, closing the doors behind them.

Dallan grinned at her merrily, his smile telling her he was alright in spite of his limp. Finn didn't look at her, focusing entirely on Brian.

Eva's heart wrenched. Perhaps he wouldn't forgive her so easily for her cold dismissal.

The men lined up before Brian, stepping forward one by one and swearing their oaths. Finn was at the end of the line.

When it was Dallan's turn, Eva couldn't help but be proud of her brother's achievement. Over fifty men had begun the trials. He was among the five who had finished them.

"I hereby swear my sword to the service of the King of Mumhain, Brian son of Mahon, lord of the Nine Kingdoms and rightful heir to the seat of Caiseal. I will do as he commands. I give him my life in service of the crown. I will help any in need. I will not base a man's treatment on his wealth or status. I will marry for love. I live to serve the people." Her brother's words were the only sound in the hall.

"I accept your oath and your sword, Dallan son of Conn. Welcome to the Fianna."

Finally, Finn stepped forward. He gave Dallan a sideways glance. Dallan nodded, an odd look passing between them. Finn took a deep breath, as though steeling himself.

"My King," he began, clearly not reciting the same oath as the others. "I must beg your forgiveness, for I will not swear an oath I cannot fulfill."

What was he doing?

"And what of my oath gives you such difficulty?" Brian asked, seemingly unperturbed by the odd turn of events.

"I cannot marry for love," he explained, his voice rough. "I've given my heart to a woman who will not marry. I can give it to no other. Therefore, I cannot fulfill that oath."

Eva nearly fell out of her chair, tipping sideways as the blood rushed from her head. Had he truly refused to join the Fianna because of her? Was this not the key to saving his sister, to helping his family? Yet here he stood, giving it all up because he loved her.

"Unless," Finn added, "she could be persuaded to reconsider."

"By Odin, man, just ask her!" Sitric shouted from the dais behind her.

Eva felt a hot blush rise to her cheeks. They were all in on it. Finn, Dallan, Brian, Sitric.

Which meant they all approved of the match.

Which meant all she had to do was say yes.

Finn walked over to her, kneeling before her chair and taking both her hands in his own. "Eva," his voice filled with emotion, "you have stolen my heart. I cannot conceive of a life lived without you, sharing joys and burdens together. Please, will you be my wife?"

The entire hall awaited her response. But Eva only saw Finn.

Falling into his arms, finally letting the tears flow, she nodded into his shoulder.
"Yes."

# CHAPTER THIRTY-SEVEN

"I NOTICED YOUR dress," Finn whispered, pulling her into his lap beneath the milky moonlight.

"It seems I didn't need it after all," Eva replied.

Following Finn's terribly public proposal, Eva decided she could speak with Sitric and her brother on the morrow. This night, she only wanted Finn.

Beneath the shade of the forest near Caiseal, Finn and Eva found solace. They wandered hand-in-hand, winding their way through the filtered moonlight until they found an old, moss-covered oak in a clearing. The midnight skies watched over them as they laid down blankets and rested under the bower.

They had kissed many times since the trials began. Some kisses had been sweet, tender. Others had been passionate and intense. This kiss was a promise. A solemn vow, a beginning to a life shared together in love.

Finn's fingers absently traced along the edge of her body, leaving a now-familiar trail of fiery desire. She had missed his kindness and his friendship, certainly. But she had also missed his touch, his embrace. Her hands pulled him toward her with urgency. She needed to be in his arms, to be joined with him in more than just words.

Finn eagerly complied. His hands worked their way under her gown, removing it with shocking swiftness. He fell upon her, heavy and warm and wonderful. And as they joined once more under the starry night sky, Eva knew that she could never again live her life in fear.

She would live it in love.

THE NEXT MORNING came all too soon. They spent the night together in each other's arms, planning a beautiful future. Now they sat, Eva in Finn's lap, his arms wrapped about her middle, watching dawn break across the still waters.

"What did you speak of with Brian last night?" Eva asked, recalling that Finn had left her side for entirely too long to speak privately with the king.

"I tested my good standing yet again," he told her with a laugh. "I asked for permission to help my sister."

Eva turned to look up at him expectantly. "What did he say? Did he allow it?"

Finn grinned, a wide smile that went through his eyes and drew her in closer.

"He gave me all the Fianna, horses, and permission to do whatever necessary to secure my family's safety, whether it be collecting the fine owed my family or exacting revenge as I see fit."

Eva smiled broadly, relief washing through her. "Oh, that's wonderful!" she cried excitedly. "When do you leave? Soon, I hope, for your sister's sake."

At mention of Ethlinn, Finn's jaw tightened. "Brian suggested that we leave this morn, and he expects us back in three days' time," Finn replied. "Is it alright that I leave so soon after our betrothal?"

"I've resigned myself to the knowledge that you will be here one day and gone the next without much warning at all. It is the life you've chosen, and the one I've agreed to. I have but one rule."

"That being?"

Eva put a gentle hand on his face, pulling him in for a soft kiss. "For every day you are gone from me, you must spend one bedding me."

"That's not a rule, love," he breathed. "That's just how it must be."

"I'LL LET YOU have the first hit," Diarmid told Finn as they rode out of Caiseal that morn, "but we'd better all get one."

"A man who treats anyone that way doesn't deserve to draw breath," Cormac added, nodding approval to his brother.

Finn shook his head, unable to believe these men were not only willing, but excited even, to avenge his sister. Never in all his wildest dreams had he imagined a life as the one he now had. A band of the fiercest men in the kingdom willing to die for each other and their king. A friend who felt closer than kin. And a woman, a princess no less, who wanted to marry him, a peasant, in spite of everything. She truly loved him, and each time he thought of it he grew more grateful for Eva.

"I'm going to speak with my family first, to get their opinion on the matter. I'm not going to kill him unless it's absolutely necessary," Finn reminded them for the hundredth time that day.

"Whether we kill him or not, that man has a beating coming for him." Dallan's tone brooked no room for dissent. "If anyone had done that to Eva, he would've been dead already. And I am happy to do the same for your sister."

They rode, passing the time threatening Ernin and jesting good-naturedly, until the sun reached its height. Finn opened his mouth to insult Diarmid, who always had one coming, honestly, when he saw horsemen approaching on the road.

Cormac held up a fist, halting the men. Seconds later, he called "It's Illadan!" and took off at a gallop toward the oncoming travelers.

Finn rode after him with Dallan by his side, hoping to hear word of his sister and better formulate his plan. When Illadan came within sight, however, Finn nearly fell off his horse.

Then he got angry.

Illadan sat *with his arms around Ethlinn,* who looked pretty damned comfortable riding in front of him on his horse. Too comfortable. Finn watched in growing horror as his baby sister looked up at Illadan with an emotion he flat-out refused to name.

Good gods, what had happened?

He swore an oath, riding right up to Illadan and Ethlinn's horse, barely registering that his parents followed them on a horse-drawn cart.

"What in the name of all the gods do you think you're doing?" he roared.

Beside him, Dallan choked on a laugh. "Now you know how it feels," he muttered, clearly not understanding how serious this was.

"Odin's balls, man," his father grumbled from the cart, "let your sister have her happiness. Gods know she deserves it."

Several of the men broke out in laughter at his father's colorful oath. Finn had forgotten how his father enjoyed those.

Cormac rode up next to Finn and Dallan, beaming at Illadan. "Are congratulations in order, then?"

Did no one see the problem here? Finn felt like everyone was going mad. His *baby sister* was…was…

Gods, he couldn't even think of it.

"Aye," Illadan replied, smiling more than Finn had ever seen him do, "Ethlinn is my wife."

Finn watched his sister turn and hug Illadan, resting her head on his chest just as Eva had done with him that morn.

And then it struck him. Ethlinn had been broken by her interactions with Ernin, far more so than Eva had been by her time as a hostage. But as he looked at her now, beaming in joy and filled with hope, Finn realized that his father was right. Ethlinn did deserve this. Had he not been riding to see to her happiness himself?

So he would do his utmost to let her have it.

Long after everyone else had offered their well wishes and

felicitations, Finn sighed. "Congratulations," he ground out, knowing it sounded forced. "I believe it will take some getting used to, but I wish you both the best."

Dallan let out a roar of laughter then, not even trying to hold it in. "Illadan, it will please you to know that Finn has just become betrothed to *my* sister. So he has, in fact, no place at all to comment on the matter."

"Is that so?" Illadan commented thoughtfully.

"Thanks, best friend," Finn grumbled tartly.

"Have no fear Ulfsson," Illadan declared, nudging his horse to continue the journey. "I still request your approval, just as I did your father's."

Finn directed his horse to ride alongside them, back in the direction of Caiseal. He had ten thousand questions, but only one really mattered. He captured Ethlinn's gaze. "Does he make you happy?"

"Aye," Ethlinn proclaimed, "very much so." Her bruises had faded, though she looked much changed from the Ethlinn he remembered some nine months' past. Stronger, more confident, content.

Finn nodded. That was enough. "Then may Frigg bless your union."

"What of the trouble with the petty lordling?" Diarmid asked, looking reluctant to turn back to Caiseal before resolving the matter.

Finn intended to question Illadan and Ethlinn over it, but as his parents traveled with them, he assumed the family had decided to leave Ath Dara and their troubles behind.

"Did he pay the fine?" Cormac asked, apparently also curious. "If not, we can continue and exact it from him."

The muscles in Illadan's jaw twitched, his arm tightening around Ethlinn. "He paid for his crimes with his life."

"And that," Cormac declared, slapping Illadan on the back approvingly, "is why you're the leader of the Fianna. Welcome home."

# CHAPTER THIRTY-EIGHT

"F INN!" HIS MOTHER called from the cart. "Come over here."

Dutifully, Finn slowed his horse until he rode beside his parents. "What is it, mother?"

"I need to hear all about this woman of yours and all the trials you went through," she told him, the pride in her voice clear. "Illadan says the tests are rigorous, that few men can complete them."

"Clearly, they are child's play for my son," his father boasted, his flaxen head held high. Finn's father, Ulf, was the only man he'd ever met who was taller than him. Even his uncle, his father's brother, was a hair shorter than Finn. But Ulf was a great man, indeed. Hearing his praise flooded Finn with warmth.

Finn swallowed, collecting his thoughts. "It's more than I can tell before we arrive," he replied. "Once we're there, Eva can help me. She's been composing a song of the trials over the past weeks, and I believe she could be persuaded to play it for you."

"Eva? This is your betrothed?" his mother's voice rose with interest.

"Aye. Eva is Dallan's sister, a princess of Laigin and war hostage of Brian."

"God's bones," his mother blurted. "You've done well for yourself, then."

Finn smiled. His mother had no idea how truly she spoke. "I have indeed."

As soon as Finn and Dallan had gone, Eva sought out Sitric.

She found him flirting with a kitchen maid. Rolling her eyes, and wondering why she was even surprised, Eva walked over to the pair of them and cleared her throat.

"May I speak with you a moment?"

Sitric grinned at her, winked at the maid, then followed Eva across the courtyard to the kitchen garden. Eva had always enjoyed strolling through the impressive garden, breathing deeply the sweet scent of nectar and the sharp tang of herbs in the summer sun. It seemed a good place for a quiet conversation.

"I'm sorry to interrupt your efforts," she began, nodding in the direction they'd come.

Sitric shrugged. "It's of no consequence. She'll still be interested tonight."

Eva pursed her lips. "Indeed."

"What is it you wished to speak of, dearest cousin?"

"I wanted to thank you," she replied earnestly. "I suspect you were involved in Finn's plotting, and I am grateful that you helped get the match approved."

"It was the least I could do in repayment for your sacrifice. And besides," Sitric bent to pick a sprig of mint, "Brian would have allowed it whether I came here or not. I am happy for you, cousin, truly. Finn is a good man and a great warrior. He will bring you honor."

Eva smiled to herself, watching as Sitric crushed the mint between his fingers, savoring its delicious scent.

"This one's always been my favorite," he chuckled. "It smells like happiness."

Eva laughed along with him. "You never cease to surprise me," she declared. "One minute you're seducing a kitchen maid, and the next you're baring your soul over an herb."

"It's important to maintain an air of mystery. To keep your

enemies guessing." He leveled her with a bemused look, one eyebrow raised.

How Eva had missed her family. She knew Sitric's company would only last a short while, and she was determined to enjoy it while she could. "If you didn't come for the wedding, why are you here?"

"Brian and I had much to discuss following Baeth's betrayal at the battle. He's created rather a mess for Morda and me to clean up."

None of this surprised Eva. Baeth was nothing but a trouble-maker. Apparently even in death. "What does he demand in recompense?"

"He tried to get me to agree to a marriage," Sitric smacked his lips in distaste at the very notion, "but I managed to talk him out of that for the time being. Instead, Morda and I will send men to bolster his forces permanently and lessen our capability for mischief."

Eva frowned. She knew her cousin better than that.

"His words," Sitric explained. "He doesn't know I need no men at all to cause mischief."

"Don't you go getting me killed," Eva warned. "Don't forget I'm here on your behalf."

Sitric waved a hand dismissively. "It will only be a *little* mischief. Not slaying-a-hostage mischief. I swear it."

"Please don't burn any more monasteries," she pleaded.

"I won't make promises I can't keep. But I promise I will avoid it, and we will leave the priests alive should we require funding."

Eva shook her head. She would never understand Sitric.

When they completed a second turn around the garden, a shadow appeared in the gate to the courtyard.

Finn.

Eva ran over to him, throwing herself into his arms and for-getting her cousin entirely. "You're back so soon?"

Finn kissed her, swift and hard. "With much news. Come,"

he took her hand. "You must meet my mother."

FINN'S MOTHER WAS positively adoring. Elan's infectious laughter filled the feasting hall as everyone sat for dinner. As the betrothed of one of the Fianna, Eva was no longer required to sit alone as a hostage. For the rest of her days, she could enjoy meals with her brother and her soon-to-be husband.

As a special treat, this particular meal Eva had the privilege of meeting Finn's entire family and hearing the tale of their struggle against Ethlinn's attacker. Illadan sat beside Ethlinn, every once in a while placing a kiss on her cheek. Eva thought it was terribly romantic, but she noted Finn's look of disgust every time Illadan touched his sister.

She supposed Dallan must feel similarly when he had to sit with her and Finn. She'd have to apologize later, and possibly tease him as well.

After meeting Finn's father, and hearing the man speak in his deep, melodious voice, Eva understood where Finn acquired his affinity for song. And she also could see where association with such a man might make it difficult to fit in, especially for someone trying to hide his heritage.

Ulf and Elan insisted on hearing every detail of their courtship, every detail fit for sharing that is. When they asked for tales from Finn's trials, Finn looked at Eva, his eyes sparkling. "My lovely Eva has just finished composing a song on just that," he proclaimed.

Eva wanted to melt into her bench. Lord, she wasn't ready to perform the thing yet. She'd only just settled on the wording a week ago. Finn knew that, of course. And he also had heard her play it many times, helping her choose the best notes and chords.

He'd spoken loud enough to catch the attention of the rest of the table, where the king's Fianna sat feasting. Every one of them—Illadan, Cormac, Broccan, Dallan, Diarmid, Conan, and Ardál—raised the cry, demanding a performance.

Eva glared daggers at her betrothed.

But Finn wouldn't back down. He leaned near, planting a kiss on her cheek and whispering in her ear, his warm breath tickling her. "They will love it. 'Tis a song worthy of the halls of kings."

Utterly mortified, with a hot flush rising up her cheeks, Eva retrieved her harp quickly and returned to the hall. Silence followed her to the bard's seat near the hearth.

Ignoring the whoosh filling her ears, Eva managed to strike the first notes. She searched the faces of the room anxiously, trying to determine if they hated it already. Once her eyes found Finn's, she never strayed. His blue eyes, the same clear, bright hue as Loch Derg, watched her with love and admiration, giving her the courage to keep going.

A serene calm filled the room, the hearth fire quietly crackling, as Eva played her song for them.

The song of the Fianna.

# About the Author

Sophia has been telling stories since she could talk. She loves learning almost as much as she loves writing, pursuing both her undergraduate and master's degrees. She has studied archaeology, anthropology, and the languages and histories of a variety of cultures. Her master's degree is in medieval history, with a focus on the British Isles. She's been fortunate enough to participate in three archaeological excavations and surveys–one at a Native American settlement in southern Indiana, one at a Tudor estate in Essex, and one at an early medieval ringfort in County Roscommon, Ireland.

After marrying her high school sweetheart, attending grad school, and moving nearly ten times in as many years, Sophia and her husband settled into a lake house in northern Indiana. When she isn't working on her next novel, you can find her in the garden and covered in dirt. They live happily in the middle of nowhere with two little boys, two atrociously rude doggos, and one ornery cat.

**Facebook:**
facebook.com/SophiaNyeWrites

**Instagram:**
instagram.com/sophianyewrites

**TikTok:**
tiktok.com/@sophianyewrites

**BookBub:**
bookbub.com/authors/sophia-nye

**Goodreads:**
goodreads.com/author/show/20815931.Sophia_Nye

**Amazon Author Page:**
amazon.com/Sophia-Nye/e/B08L9XZ148

**Website:**
sophianyewrites.com

www.ingramcontent.com/pod-product-compliance
Lightning Source LLC
Chambersburg PA
CBHW060411310726
48976CB00003B/1013